Jim Henson

Young Puppeteer

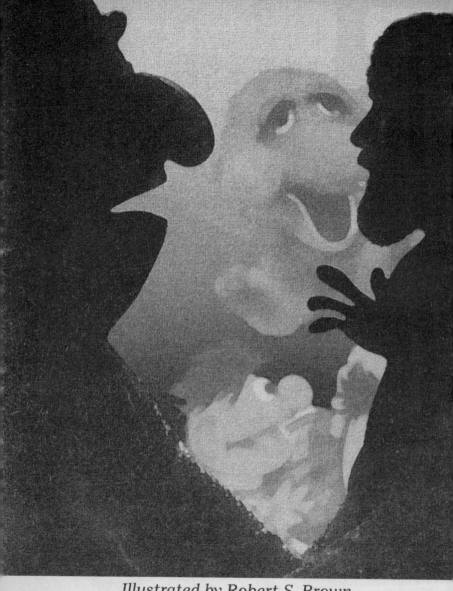

Illustrated by Robert S. Brown

Jim Henson

Young Puppeteer

by Leslie Gourse

ALADDIN PAPERBACKS

New York London Toronto Sydney Singapore

First Aladdin Paperbacks edition May 2000

Text copyright © 2000 by Leslie Gourse
Illustrations copyright © 2000 by Robert S. Brown

Aladdin Paperbacks
An imprint of Simon & Schuster Children's Publishing Division
1230 Avenue of the Americas
New York, NY 10020

The text for this book was set in Adobe Garamond
Printed and bound in the United States of America.
2 4 6 8 10 9 7 5 3 1

Library of Congress Cataloging-in-Publication Data
Gourse, Leslie.
Jim Henson: young puppeteer / by Leslie Gourse.—
1st Aladdin Paperbacks ed.
p.   cm.—(Childhood of famous Americans)
Summary: A biography of Jim Henson,
the famous puppeteer and creator of the Muppets.
ISBN 0-689-83398-9
1. Henson, Jim—Juvenile literature. 2. Puppeteers—United States—
Biography—Juvenile literature. [1. Henson, Jim. 2. Puppeteers.]
I. Title. II. Series
PN1982.H46 G68   2000   791.5'3'092—dc21
[B] 99-052607

Illustrations

Contents

Jim Henson

Young Puppeteer

Jim Henson Is Born in Mississippi

The dark night was so quiet in the tiny hamlet of Stoneville, Mississippi, that the only sound you could hear was the croaking of frogs in nearby Deer Creek. Paul Henson, Sr., was reading reports on the research he was doing on soybeans. The U.S. Department of Agriculture had stationed him in its laboratory and offices in Stoneville. Betty Henson was resting on the couch, listening to a radio program, in the living room next door to her husband's den. And two-year-old Paul Henson, Jr., was asleep in his crib in his bedroom.

"Mmmmm," Betty said under her breath.

Her husband looked up quickly. "Are you all right?" he called.

"Yes, dear . . . but it's time. The baby's coming."

"Okay, let's go to the hospital!" he said, and went to their bedroom for his wife's little overnight bag. He also went to their first child's room, picked up Paul, Jr., wrapped him in a blanket, and hurried with his wife and baby to their old car right outside the front porch of their house.

The headlights went on, illuminating the pitch-black road. Paul Henson, Sr., drove as fast as his little old car could go along Deer Creek Road for the nine-mile trip to Leland, and then he kept heading straight to Greenville, the biggest city in the area. The bright lights of the Kings Daughter Hospital reassured him. Help was at hand. Medical workers came out to get her. And within a few minutes of reaching the delivery room, Betty Henson gave birth to her second child, on September 24, 1936.

A nurse came out of the delivery room to give the news to Paul, who was sitting on the edge of a chair, holding Paul, Jr., in his arms. The baby was crying. Dad hadn't stopped in the kitchen to bring anything for him to drink. The nurse said, "Your wife and son are doing fine."

"Oh, wonderful," the new father said, and leaned back in the chair.

"Let me bring you a glass of juice for your son here," said the nurse.

"Thanks so much," said Paul.

In those days, doctors usually kept new mothers and their babies for at least a week in the hospital. But as soon as Betty Henson saw her husband that night, she said, "Let's go home now. I feel fine. You know how I feel. I don't really feel comfortable in a hospital." She was a Christian Scientist.

"No," her husband said, "you have to stay here for a while."

They decided to name their new son James Maury Henson. Within a couple of days, the doctors decided to let her go home, and she was riding in the car beside her husband, holding James Maury Henson in her arms. In the bright sunlight, she was smiling, relaxed. "Aren't the cypress trees beautiful," she said about the hundreds of trees dotting the landscape. "And the flowers are gorgeous," she added about the bright pink, red, and white flowers that seemed to grow wild everyplace. "That old frame house looks wonderful to me," she said to her husband. They drove to the front steps of their home.

On the porch stood "Dear," Betty's mother, holding Paul, Jr., 's hand, keeping him upright on his wobbly legs. He was still toddling and he needed help if he tried to get up and down the steep front steps. "Oh, Mother's taking charge of Paul. How nice of her. Well, I'll just pitch right in. I'm feeling fine," Betty said.

"Take it easy now for a while, honey. You

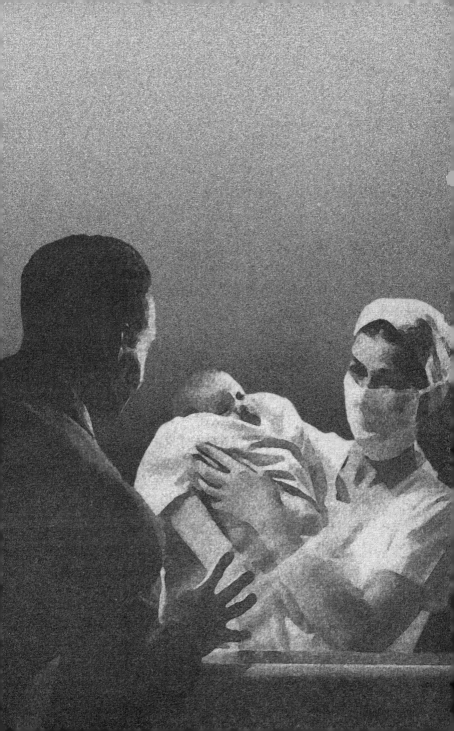

promised the doctor. You promised me, too, you know, or I wouldn't have brought you home so soon."

Betty smiled and got out of the car, holding her new son. "Dear, this is Jimmy," Betty said. She handed the newborn to her mother. Then Betty took Paul, Jr., 's hand and said, "Did you miss Mommy? I missed you."

Paul cried for a second, then stopped and smiled, holding his mother's hand. And Dear, Jimmy, and Paul, Sr., trailed the new mother and Paul, Jr., into the house. It was becoming brighter and more humid by the minute in that flat Delta territory twelve miles from the Mississippi River. The birds were singing. Not the crows, of course. They were cawing their praises of the morning.

"Don't you mind those old crows," Dear said to Jimmy. His face started to scrunch up.

"They're purple grackles, Dear," Betty said.

"You can call them anything you like, but they're still crows," Dear said. And to Jimmy she

16

added, "Aren't they, sweetheart, aren't they? Grandma's little sweetheart."

"Home sweet home with my little family," said Paul, Sr., "and the tires didn't blow out! What luck."

For a while he watched the women giving the babies their bottles and changing their diapers in the nursery room. Then he said, "Well, I think I'll go to the lab for a while, see what's going on. Will you be all right now?"

"Fine," Dear said.

"Fine," said Betty. "You've been wonderful. And we have the office number if we need anything, Paul."

"I'll come back for lunch," he said. The tall, slender man kissed Betty, Dear, Jimmy, and Paul, went out to the car, and drove off to the lab not far away.

Early Family Relationships & Childhood Games

Jimmy's earliest memories were of the sweet smell of the crepe myrtle—white-, red-, pink-, and fuschia-colored flowers that bloomed throughout the area—and the pretty sight of the cypress and pecan trees, and the sounds of nature—the birds singing in the trees, and the frogs and fish splashing in the creek. Turtles and snakes lived in the creek, too. They crept or slithered cunningly into sight, surprising him with their silent approaches, when he first started to walk around in the yard or near the creek. Dear often took him for walks to the creek. And in the mornings, everyone awakened to the birdcalls. Some were melodious songs. But others sounded like the twanging of taut wires. Jimmy was curious about all of the creatures.

Jimmy came to love the animals, and he began to draw them. He also cut pictures of birds out of magazines and pasted them into his private notebook.

Stoneville was a tiny town, with only about two hundred people living there. All of them were connected by their jobs to the agricultural center. In such a small town, there were few activities for children. He had to find ways to entertain himself. Animals are what held his interest. Soon Jimmy grew old enough to walk steadily on his feet and he could hold a little fishing rod. So Jimmy's father took him along with his brother, Paul, fishing in the creek at night. Other men went there with their sons, too. Sometimes even the wives and daughters went to fish. They whispered "hello" to each other, trying to keep their voices down so they wouldn't scare away the fish. Nighttime was the best time to catch fish. The men and boys caught turtles, too. Jimmy's father let him keep the turtles as pets—and even some of the snakes. All of them were harmless around there. And so Jimmy never felt afraid of the wildlife around the creek.

Paul, Jr., didn't particularly like to keep animals as pets. He preferred to tinker with little toys that their parents bought when they went shopping in Leland. A little bit farther away, the bigger city of Greenville had a fine toy store. Jimmy's parents bought him sketch pads and brightly colored crayons because they saw how much he loved to draw animals and birds. Not only did Jimmy like to draw the birds he saw in the area, he also made up designs for all kinds of exotic-looking birds—green ones with huge beaks, and pink-colored and brown-striped ones with blue markings on their wings, and beaks like curlicues.

His mother seemed impressed with his work, but she always seemed too busy with chores to do in the house to really pay attention. She knew how to can fruit, berries, and vegetables to preserve them for the winter. She liked to bake her own bread, muffins, cakes, and pies. Sometimes the wives of other scientists at the center came to the house for muffins and tea. Betty often showed her guests the little constructions Paul, Jr., made with blocks and wires.

Both Paul, Jr., and Jimmy received the gift of a toy train set. But Paul spent more time than Jimmy did playing with it. Jimmy liked to watch the trains go in and out of tunnels and over hills. But for the most part, he assisted his brother, or sat aside, drawing his animals and birds. Or he played with his frogs on the front porch. He liked to let them jump around. Then he caught them just before they skittered down the steps and disappeared under the house and back into the wild. He let his turtles out of the little wire mesh houses he constructed for them.

Sometimes a frog got loose in the house and surprised Betty by jumping up at her when she went to use the vacuum cleaner. Or she or Dear would find a turtle sleeping on a chair just in the nick of time before they sat down.

"Jimmy, please pull that turtle out of here!" Betty would call out to him. Or, "Jimmy, please keep your frogs out on the porch!" But Betty wasn't timid around animals and, laughing at her discoveries, she would pick them up and put them out the front door herself.

Jimmy's grandmother, Dear, usually sat on a rocking chair on the high porch and laughed at the antics of Jimmy and his pets. She liked to watch Jimmy chase the frogs and retrieve them from under the porch or on their way to the groves of trees that stood between the house and Deer Creek. Dear sometimes helped him. She was very proud of herself when she caught a frog with her own bare hands.

"See how quick I still am!" she would say with a laugh.

"Did you used to have frogs as pets?" he asked.

"No," she said. "I liked grasshoppers. But I never kept them for long, because they got too sleepy in bottles."

Jimmy noticed that Dear liked to paint pictures of animals, too. She read magazines that came to the house by subscription—*Collier's, The Saturday Evening Post,* and *The Saturday Review,* among other popular magazines in those days. Sometimes she read magazine stories aloud to Jimmy. He liked to sit on the porch steps and listen to her. Very often he did the talking while his grandmother sat quietly, listening to him and working with her hands. She created patchwork quilts from a large pile of squares and triangles of printed cloth that she collected. Some squares had flowers and birds and little squiggles of abstract designs on them. They looked like rags. But when she stitched them together, they became as pretty as tapestries. Betty actually hung one on a wall for decoration.

Dear also knitted, crocheted, and embroidered flowers and birds and leaves onto squares and rectangles of perforated material. All of her creations went into use in the house as blankets and pillow covers and even place mats at the dining table. Jimmy had a knitted blanket she made with bluebirds and green leaves all over it on his bed.

Whenever Jimmy or Paul, Jr., caught colds, or had stomachaches, or felt sick at all, the family didn't call a doctor to visit the house. Instead, Dear usually came to the rescue. She put cold compresses on their heads when they had fevers. Once, both Jimmy and Paul, Jr., became covered with an itchy, red rash. Dear told them it was poison ivy. She took them to the place near the creek where the three-pronged, shiny red poison ivy leaves grew near the base of a tree. She said to the boys, "You must learn to recognize the plants and stay away from them." She gave them tiny white little pills that tasted like mints.

"Candy pills," she said playfully. "These will help." She then told them about God's loving care for them, unconditional and permanent.

Paul, Sr., seeing his sons scratch their rashes from poison ivy, went to town and brought back a bottle of a pinkish-white liquid.

He told them: "This is calamine lotion. My mother used to put it on me when I had poison ivy. You'll feel much better."

He smeared it over the boys, even though Dear didn't want him to do it.

She said, "They'll get better without it."

But the calamine lotion *did* help relieve the rashes.

When Paul, Jr., started to go away to school every morning in nearby Leland, Betty sometimes drove him. Parents of all the children took turns driving from Stoneville to the public school in Leland and picking them up in the afternoons. Paul brought homework back with him. Betty helped him learn to spell and do simple additions. She also encouraged him about his penmanship, teaching him the correct way to hold his pencil. Jimmy watched, fascinated. He didn't know how to write his own name yet. But Paul could make looping letters very carefully with a little slant to the right.

Then Jimmy would find Dear sitting alone, doing her needlework. He asked her, "When can I go to school?"

She said, "You'll be going soon. Then I'll be sitting here, waiting for both of you to come home and tell me what you've been doing."

In the meantime, she was always eager to look at his drawings and listen to his ideas about how he would go to school in Leland. "I'll learn to sign my name to my drawings the way real artists do," he told her.

"That will be wonderful," Dear said. "You'll be one of the best, if you keep at it. I can already see you have talent."

"When will I go to school?" he asked her nearly every day.

"Soon," Dear always said. "You'll be going in September. You and Paul will go together in the mornings."

"Will I be good at school?" Jim said. "Is it hard?"

"No, Jimmy, it will be fun for you. You're so smart, like Paul is. You'll paint pictures and make friends with the other children. You'll sit in a room with lots of little desks and chairs. A teacher will stand in front of the class and tell you stories. She'll show you how to write your name. And she'll look at what you draw. You'll be the best artist in the class. I already know that, because you have a lot of talent for painting and drawing."

"Will you come to school with me?" Jimmy said. "I don't want to leave you."

"No, you sweet thing, you'll go with Paul. He'll take you to your classroom before he goes to his. Afterward, you can come home together and tell me all about what you did all day and what your teachers are like."

"Suppose I have trouble with the school-work," Jimmy said.

"Just try as hard as you can and always do your best. And that's the way to do well in school."

Sometimes when Paul came home from school, he took Jimmy with him to the creek. They went swimming together. And their cousins, the sons of their mother's sister, Agnes, and her husband, nicknamed Jinx, visited Stoneville occasionally and went along. All the boys could feel the fish slithering past their legs. Sometimes something seemed to nibble at their toes a little, too. When the fish swam close to the surface of the water, Jimmy could actually see the distinct outlines of the catfish and the bream, which were also called "blue-gills." It was fun to be close enough to be able to tell the difference between the catfish and the bluegills in the murky water. The boys laughed, giggled together, raced, and splashed each other.

Both of the Henson boys were skinny and wiry with long, bony faces. Jimmy resembled his grandmother Dear. Paul, of course, was taller than Jimmy, but Jimmy could run and swim nearly as far and as fast as Paul. When they had races, usually Paul won because his arms and legs were longer.

Afterward, they lay down on their backs beneath the cypress trees at the side of the creek and looked up at the sky, telling each other what kinds of clouds they were looking at—fleecy, fluffy cumulus clouds, and little specks of cirrus, and long, thin stratus, and gray, lumpy, nimbus clouds. Their father had taught them the differences between the clouds. All the while, Jimmy listened to the *glug glug* sound of the frogs as the light began to fade. And he dreamed for a day when he would grow up to be tall; he wanted to be six foot three, he decided. His dream would come true, but he had no way of knowing that then. He didn't like being the smallest one in the family.

Once he told Paul about his wish. "If only I could grow to be real tall. Do you think I will?"

Paul said comfortingly, "Yes, you probably will."

Jimmy said, "And I want to do something important one day."

"So do I," said Paul, "like Daddy does."

Sometimes the brothers fought, as all brothers do, and Paul began making friends his own age. Jimmy didn't know them. But most of the time the brothers got along very well and were close friends. Before the sun set altogether, the boys gathered pecans that fell off the trees and brought them home to their mother. She made delicious, creamy smooth, sweet pecan pies, which she served with a dollop of ice cream for special treats.

Early School Days

Sometimes their father took the boys to the laboratory at Stoneville and let them walk around and look at all the test tubes, the experiments, and the sacks of soybeans. He was doing research with soybean seed breeding to improve them. As a coworker of Paul Henson's would recall years later, "Soybeans weren't growing too much in the south at that time." Father put on a white coat over his shirt and pants and went to work himself. The boys loved to see him looking through a microscope at little slides. He let them look through his microscope.

"What's that for?" Paul, Jr., often asked.

"Why do you wear an apron?" Jimmy wanted to know.

"So Mother doesn't have to work too hard to get my clothes clean," their father said. "She has enough work with you kids."

Many different scientists were doing different types of experiments. Jimmy saw some people working with cotton, and others with pecans, and others with all kind of plants, vegetables, fruit, and trees. One of the scientists was a very good friend of the Henson family. His name was Buford Williamson, and he had just come to town to work on research about the mechanization of cotton production. His wife used to go to Betty Henson's house for tea and small talk.

Before Buford Williamson started his job at Stoneville, he did a favor for the Hensons. Paul, Sr., wanted Buford to build a tennis court for Paul, Jr., and Jimmy to play on. Buford was happy to build it, and once it was finished, he liked to watch the boys volley the balls back and forth to each other. They were very active, healthy kids, he thought. Not only the Henson kids but everyone at Stoneville started playing tennis on the court. It became a very popular pasttime in that small community with so few other diversions.

When Buford started working at Stoneville, he noticed how smart and curious the Henson boys were about everything. Buford thought the Henson family might have come from Oklahoma. If they hadn't been born there, they may have just worked there before being sent to the lab at Stoneville by the U.S. Department of Agriculture. The Henson boys were typical children of a scientist. They were always asking questions about the research being done. "They're downright nosy!" Buford said with a laugh to a friend.

By that time, Jimmy was going to school, too. He traveled with his brother, Paul, along Deer Creek Road, the one connection between Stoneville and Leland, to the Leland Grammar

School. Even though he was a quiet child, Jimmy began to make quite a few friends. All of them were white boys and girls. Leland was a completely segregated town in those days, with about five thousand people, half of whom were African American. None of the African Americans went to Jimmy's school.

One of the white boys in Jimmy's class was named Gordon Jones. Gordon provided Jimmy with some of his only information about the African Americans in the Leland area. Gordon lived on his family's farm near Stoneville, and he had African American friends, farmers' children, too, with whom he played baseball and other games. He happened to tell Jimmy one day about a wonderful baseball pitcher.

Jimmy asked Gordon about his playmates in the farmland around Leland. "What are they like? Are they different from us?"

Gordon said, "Now, they're another color, that's all. You can come and play with us anytime."

Jimmy nodded and thought about it. "I'll

have to ask my father to drive me to your farm one day."

"Sure, you do that," Gordon said. "Or you could come by horseback. We play after the chores are done. And sometimes we play on Sundays after church."

Jimmy laughed. "We don't have any horses."

"Oh," Gordon said. "I have my own pony."

Jimmy's father was always busy working during the afternoons. By the time he came home, it was too late for him to take Jimmy to go play baseball. Betty had dinner ready. So instead of going to the Gordon family farm, Jimmy waited for Gordon to come to Stoneville. So on Saturday afternoons, Gordon sometimes rode his pony to Jimmy's house, and the boys went swimming in the creek. Gordon's pony made him independent. Jimmy liked that idea. A car could make a person independent, but he knew he was too young to have a car.

Jimmy also became friendly with a boy named Royal Frazier, who was born in the same hospital in Greenville as Jimmy had been. But Royal had been born on November 6, 1936. He was two months younger than Jimmy. Sometimes Royal, who lived in Leland, went to Jimmy's house on Saturdays, too, and swam in the creek with Jimmy and Paul, Jr., and Gordon.

The boys became friendly and started visiting each other when they were in the second grade. But then Jimmy's father gave his children a big surprise. One night at dinner Paul, Sr., said, "We'll be moving to Hyattsville, Maryland, soon. The Department of Agriculture wants me to go work there."

"Where's Maryland?" Jimmy said. "Can I still go to the same school?"

"No, no," his father said. "It's quite a distance from here. Hyattsville, Maryland, is right near Washington, D.C. That's the nation's capital city. You know that, don't you?"

"I think so," Jimmy said, and looked at his brother Paul.

"Sure, I know that," Paul said. "I've heard of

Washington. That's where the president lives."

"President who?" said their father.

"President Roosevelt," said Paul, Jr.

"President Franklin Delano Roosevelt," said their father.

"President Franklin Delano Roosevelt," said the boys together.

"Very good!" said their father.

"Excellent!" said their mother.

"Gold stars for everyone," said Dear.

"You'll go to school in Hyattsville," their father said. "You'll like it. It will be a much bigger place. And you'll see all the important government buildings in Washington. You'll have a real education."

Jimmy had to tell his schoolmates that his family was moving to Washington, D.C. Most of them had never heard of it, or they had heard of it but didn't know what it was. Quickly, it seemed to Jimmy, his mother and Dear packed all their belongings. Men came to help them move boxes into a big truck, and everyone drove north to Hyattsville, Maryland, near Washington.

Jimmy and Paul started going to school in suburban Hyattsville, a small town but not so small and rural as Leland. There was no creek. Everyone had telephones in Hyattsville. Nobody had to wind them up to make a phone call (like the old-fashioned telephone Jimmy's family had had), and nobody had a party line, the way some people did in Leland and Stoneville. A party line meant two and sometimes three different families shared the same phone number. Each family had a different number of rings to signal that a call was coming in. When one family, or party, got a call, the other people on the party line had to wait for the call to end. Then another person could make or receive a call. Dear went to live with the Hensons in Hyattsville, too. And occasionally some of their cousins visited.

Jimmy was really impressed when his parents took him from Maryland to nearby Washington, D.C., and showed him the historic sights there. One was the graceful mansion called the White House, on Pennsylvania Avenue. President Roosevelt, his wife, Eleanor, and their five children lived there. Another beautiful building was the Capitol building, with its huge, round dome. That's where the Senate and the House of Representatives had their chambers, and the legislators voted about the laws of the country. In another building, part of the Smithsonian Institution, Jimmy saw a huge painting called *The Last Supper,* by Salvador Dali, a Spanish artist. It depicted Jesus and his Apostles dining together. Jimmy also saw the Library of Congress and the Supreme Court building.

Their parents also took Jimmy and Paul to see the massive statue of Abraham Lincoln seated and appearing to be lost in thought, in the Lincoln Memorial. Their father recited the Gettysburg address and told the boys how important that speech was. President Lincoln had said that the world would not pay much attention or remember for very long what had happened there—a battle to preserve the Union of the Northern and Southern states with the hope of ending the Civil War. When the war did end, the slaves were freed. Lincoln had not wanted government of the people, by the people, and for the people to vanish from the earth, he wrote in his speech. It became world famous, and Lincoln was wrong: *Everyone* remembered what he had said there. The boys hadn't read that address yet in school. So they were very attentive when their father told them the story of Lincoln, the Civil War, and the occasion for the Gettysburg address. Jimmy felt very lucky to have such an educated father to teach him about the world. And the boys were very mystified and intrigued by the tall, skinny sculpture called the Washington Monument.

There was much more to do in Hyattsville, too, Jimmy noticed. Everybody had radios and could tune in to a lot of stations. He even heard about the latest invention called television. It was like a radio except you could actually see pictures on a screen. But Jimmy didn't actually see a television set. Nobody in his neighorhood owned one.

Then came another surprise. Only a few months after they moved to Hyattsville, their father told them they were going to move back to Stoneville, Mississippi. The U.S. Department of Agriculture was transferring him again. So the family packed all their belongings and drove south to their new home. It was a short distance from the house they had first lived in. The new one looked pretty much like the old one: a simple, one-story, wood frame house. But the new one had a bigger front porch, and it wrapped around two sides of the house. Almost immediately Jimmy ran to the creek, went swimming, and looked for frogs and turtles, snakes and fish. They were still there. He couldn't tell which ones had been his old pets, of course. But he felt very happy to be back with the familiar animals. He liked seeing the birds fly around and listening to

them sing. And he enjoyed the sight of the cypress trees bending over, laden with leaves, and the pecans lying on the ground and waiting to be scooped up for pies.

A couple of days after the family returned to Stoneville, Jimmy showed up at the Leland Grammar School to start classes again. His old friends remembered him. Jimmy felt as if he had never been away. Even so, in the schoolyard on his first day back, Gordon Jones and Jimmy started to argue in the school yard.

The fight started when Gordon said, "You didn't grow bigger at all. You're still too skinny."

"I am not," Jimmy said, "I'm going to be tall one day, and strong too. I'm going to fight you right now!"

Gordon laughed at Jimmy. Gordon was taller than Jimmy at that time, and Gordon had developed some muscles from his farm chores. Both of them made fists and threatened to hit each other. They pretended to throw punches, but their fists never touched each other. Both boys backed away before either of them actually could reach out far enough to strike the other one.

Jimmy said, "I'm going to get my brother, Paul, to beat you up. He'll give you a real licking. And he's twice as big as I am."

Suddenly Gordon got a tight, frightened feeling in his stomach. But he didn't run away or say he was scared. Then he and Jimmy let their hands drop and walked away from each other. The next day at school, Gordon asked Royal Frazier to point to Paul, Jr., in the hallways. Royal did it. Gordon saw that Paul, Jr., was taller than Jimmy, but skinny, too.

In the school yard that day, Gordon asked Jimmy, "When's your brother going to come and try to beat me up?"

Jimmy said, "Aw, forget about that. I didn't tell him. He might really hurt you. And he's busy building a radio, anyway."

"A radio?" Gordon said. "Can I listen to it?"

Jimmy smiled. "If it works, we can all listen. I'm helping him."

So the fight never happened. Gordon and Jimmy never threatened to hit each other again. They became friends again from that day on.

Gordon and Royal Frazier went to Jimmy's house often. Jimmy's mother was very nice to the boys. She gave them milk and cookies, and she showed them pictures of Paul and Jimmy when they were babies. In one photograph, one of Jimmy's feet looked blurred. He had moved a foot when the picture was being taken. It looked as though he had six toes on that foot.

Mrs. Henson said to the boys, "I'll bet you didn't know that Jimmy has six toes."

Royal was very surprised that Jimmy had six toes, and Jimmy had to take off his shoes and prove to Royal there were only five toes. Mrs. Henson laughed heartily. Royal never forgot that.

Many years later, Jim Henson's wife, Jane, would explain the type of jokes that the Henson family loved: "When you're in church and something doesn't happen correctly, you fall apart laughing—you can't stop. There's something about imperfection in the middle of all that. . . . I think it's a quality that was always part of the Muppets." (The Muppets would be puppets that Jim Henson would create when he grew to be a man. And he would feature them in poignant, funny, and educational television shows, commercials, and even in movies.)

When they were children, Royal noticed that Paul and Jimmy were always making things. They built model airplanes. They constructed a crystal radio set. When they finished it, it picked up programs from one radio station in Greenville nearby. Their father gave them advice about how to build many things. Then Paul, Jr., led the way, while Jimmy helped him build the radio.

Paul was a star in the sciences. Jimmy had many talents, Royal noticed. Jimmy wrote a poem about Columbus Day, with a line that said something like: "I might live in England, and you might live in France one day." Royal thought that Jimmy wrote the line especially for another of their friends, Tom Baggett, a classmate, who had a French last name.

Tom Baggett, too, went to Jimmy's house some days. And Tom was very impressed with Jimmy's fascination with birds. Jimmy had a big book, bigger than any book Tom had ever seen before—an Audubon book—that contained many pictures of birds. "You've got just about anything that flies," Tom commented.

"Yeah," Jimmy said. "My favorite bird is a purple grackle." He showed Tom a picture of one.

Tom laughed and said, "That's nothing but a common blackbird!"

"It's a purple grackle!" Jimmy said. He loved the name of the bird when he said it.

Tom laughed, but he was impressed, anyway, with how many notebooks Jimmy filled up with pictures of birds he had cut out of magazines and pasted up in his private collection.

And so the Hensons settled down to a quiet life in the beautiful, natural surroundings of Stoneville.

Cub Scout Projects with Puppets

Leland had a Cub Scout den for boys Jimmy's age. Each year, a different mother led the local den. The first year Jimmy went back to live in Stoneville, his mother was invited to lead the Cub Scouts. Gordon Jones, Royal Frazier, and Tom Baggett were in the troop with Jim and other boys. They got together at Jimmy's house, where Betty Henson served them pecan pie and milk and told them about the moral obligations of the Cub Scouts. She taught them about the value of physical activities and fair play. The boys liked to meet at Jimmy's house for their den meetings because the Hensons were so friendly. Paul Henson, Sr., liked to ask the boys questions about what they did in school, and how they felt about their teachers, and what they didn't like, and how they thought school could be improved. Would the boys like to go to school in summer and have the school closed all winter? Paul Henson asked. The boys thought that was a very amusing idea.

"It's just a joke," Paul Henson, Sr., said. "We like jokes here."

Every year, each Cub Scout was supposed to do one major project of his own invention. Jimmy didn't know what to choose to do. He asked his mother, "What shall I do?"

Betty said, "That's up to you, dear. You have to be creative and think of something for yourself. I can't do it for you."

Dear told him the same thing. Jimmy was perplexed.

At school, Jimmy asked Gordon Jones what he suggested.

Gordon said, "I don't know what I'm going to to do myself. So how can I tell you?"

"Well, maybe we can do something together," Jimmy said.

"Like what?" Gordon said.

"Maybe we could dance or sing," Jimmy said.

"I can't dance or sing. Can you?"

"No," Jim said.

"And I don't want to, anyway," Gordon said. "We'll just make fools of ourselves."

"You're right," Jimmy said. "I've got a better idea. We can do a comedy routine. We can be a team."

"Okay," Gordon said. "We can get a joke book in a store and try to make people laugh."

"You're good at telling stories," Jimmy said. "You tell jokes, and I'll stand behind you and make funny signals with my hands. Come to my house and we'll practice in front of a mirror. I'll show you what I mean."

So the boys went to Jimmy's house and stood in front of a big mirror in Jimmy's parents' room. Jimmy stood behind Gordon and slipped his arms under Gordon's. "Put your hands in your pockets," Jimmy said. Gordon did as he was told. In the mirror it looked like Jimmy's arms were Gordon's.

"Now tell some jokes," Jimmy instructed.

"Okay. Did you hear about the kidnapping down the street?"

"No, really? I didn't know about it. What happened?"

Gordon said, "He woke up."

Jimmy took a handkerchief and whacked Gordon in the face with it while Gordon kept his own hands buried in his pockets and out of sight. Gordon kept telling jokes. Jimmy prompted him. And each time Gordon told a punch line, Jimmy whacked him in the face with the handkerchief.

When the night came for the Cub Scouts to put on a display of their projects, Gordon and

Jimmy did their skit. Royal Frazier would always recall how funny it was. All the kids in the audience kept howling with laughter, especially when Jimmy hit Gordon after his punch lines. Even Paul, Jr., loved the skit, and so did both of the Baggett boys and all the parents who attended the show put on in the Leland Grammar School auditorium. They were a hit!

The next year, Jessie Mae Baggett, the mother of Jack, who was four years younger than Jimmy, and Jack's brother Tom, about two years older than Jimmy, led the Cub Scout den. She assigned the task of finding a special project to each boy in the den.

And she said to Jimmy, "I remember how much fun your skit was last year. What would you like to do this year?"

"I don't know," Jimmy said. "I'll have to think about it."

A few days later she told him she thought his skit the previous year with his hands had been so much fun that she wanted him to do something with his hands again. She thought the whole den should become involved and put on a show with puppets.

Jimmy said, "That's a good idea. I saw some hand puppets in the toy store in town."

He had been listening to *The Edgar Bergen and Charlie McCarthy Show* on the radio every week, and he thought they were very funny. Jimmy's parents and the parents of several of the other boys bought a few hand puppets in the toy store in Greenville. Some mothers made hand puppets out of dolls and material they had in their houses. And the boys got together and invented some kind of story for the puppets. Mr. Baggett, Jessie Mae's husband, built a set for the puppet show. Its stage was made out of a dark brown, Masonite board, and it had cloth curtains that parted when the show started, then came together at the end of the first act and then again at the end of the whole show.

Years later nobody could recall what the show had been about, but the puppets made it a very different sort of project than the Cub Scouts had ever done before. Jack Baggett thought the puppets could have been Jimmy's idea at the start, or Jimmy may have invented the story for the puppets. But all the Cub Scouts in the troop took part in the show. Each one had a hand puppet of his own. Jimmy didn't appear to have more talent than anybody else. He was just one of the kids, all his friends recalled. But Tom Baggett would always think that Jimmy got his start working with puppets in Leland's Cub Scout den.

Another year, Royal Frazier's mother led the Scouts. Jimmy may have worked one hand puppet by himself for his project. Nobody recalled what the shows were about. But everyone remembered the games that the Cub Scouts played when they had free time. In the summer afternoons, the boys still went swimming and frog hunting together. At night they fished in the creek. And they played with rubber guns. Jimmy, Paul, Royal Frazier, Gordon Jones—

everyone played with those toy guns. Tom Baggett would always recall exactly how they made them.

"You took an inner tube," Tom Baggett said, "cut it up, took a piece of wood and carved it into a gun shape with a big, long barrel. Then the back of the gun handle had a clothespin on it. That's what you strapped the end of the rubber onto, then hooked it over the front of the gun. Then you had the inner tube band strung out and under tension. To make the gun go off, all you did was mash the handle, and the clothespin went off. The inner tube shot off the front end of the gun."

"We didn't have real guns. This was just a kid's toy. But we used the guns for little bitty wars. We zapped each other. Everybody would have these things loaded up and catch someone coming around the side of a house. When the rubber band came out of the gun, it would sting you if it popped you on the butt. You couldn't buy these things. They were just little guns with

inner tubes that we used as the ammunition."

The boys liked to play tennis on the court that Buford Williamson had built for them. They also roller-skated on the tennis court with the nets taken down. And they played hockey with sticks and flattened tin cans. "We were a bunch of southern boys who had never seen a hockey game," Tom Baggett would remember. But they didn't let their inexperience stop them from trying to play and having a good time with their own rules.

Jimmy was never interested in fighting, and he never learned how to use a real gun and go hunting with some of the other boys in the crowd. He liked to join in sports, though he never was a ringleader and never insisted that the boys get together for a game. He just went along with the others and joined in the crowd's fun. Though he remained quiet and had a very quiet voice, he loved to be with people and join in group activities.

T. Kermit Scott
Moves to Town

When the group of friends went into the fifth grade, a new boy moved to Leland and became part of the crowd. His name was T. Kermit Scott, and he would recall becoming especially friendly with Jimmy. For Jimmy, there was one thing very intriguing about Kermit: his name. Jimmy would never forget it. But at the time they were playing together, neither Kermit nor Jimmy had any idea that Jimmy would use Kermit's name one day for a television show called *Sesame Street*. It would make Kermit's name world famous as the name of a charming and versatile hand puppet—Kermit the Frog.

Neither Jimmy nor Kermit had heard very much about television, and they had never seen a television show.

Kermit knew, however—even when they were eleven years old—that Jimmy wanted to become an entertainer. Jimmy had great dreams about that, Kermit realized, though Jimmy didn't know any of the details about how he would do it. Kermit Scott, like Jimmy, was a bit of an outsider in that flat Delta region of Mississippi. Neither of the boys had their roots solidly in Mississippi soil. For one thing, their parents had come from elsewhere. Kermit considered Jimmy to be already a bit of an intellectual and not exactly typical of the kids in Leland.

"That's real backwoods, or it was in those days, and a pretty rough place," Kermit would reflect years later. "Boys were expected to be tough." Jimmy preferred drawing and collecting animals to hunting and shooting them. Like the other boys, Kermit noticed that Jimmy didn't even go hunting once.

Kermit believed that he, too, would do something very intellectual in life. Eventually he became a philosophy professor and spent thirty-three years as a teacher at Purdue University in West Lafayette, Indiana. He thought that, as children, he and Jimmy became friends easily because both of them were academically inclined. One of their boyhood friends would become a career military man, and another would become a financial world professional— bright, practical people. But Kermit and Jimmy were both dreamers.

Jimmy particularly liked to dress up in all sorts of costumes. He persuaded Kermit to join him in the costumes, and they put on little shows in Jimmy's backyard. Kermit spent a lot of time playing theatrical games with Jimmy. Often their costumes were simply sheets that Jimmy took from his mother's linen closet. The boys wrapped themselves up in the sheets and pretended to be Indian fakirs. Sometimes they built tents by spreading the sheets over the chairs set out for people to sit in in the sun in Jimmy's yard. Jimmy's imagination ran to Eastern, exotic fantasies.

Between Jimmy's house and the creek lay a field. Gordon Jones once brought his pony to Jimmy's house while Kermit was playing there. Both Jimmy and Kermit took turns riding the pony. It threw both of them off. That made a big impression on Kermit, and he thought it did on Jimmy, too. Kermit didn't ride the pony more than that one time. But Jimmy kept trying, no matter how many times he was thrown off, until he finally learned to ride.

Once he learned, he bought a horse named Peggy from a neighbor. The horse liked to run close to the trees so that the branches pushed people off her back. The Hensons didn't have a stable or a special place for Peggy to live in, so they simply left her outside the house.

They had plenty of space there for the horse.

Kermit thought that Jimmy even looked a little like a horse. Jimmy had a long face, and he had a loping walk. That gait reminded Kermit of a horse. Jimmy looked like a country bumpkin type, Kermit thought, though of course Kermit knew that Jimmy wasn't like that at all. He was a soft-spoken, even-tempered, and peaceable fellow who kept his head in a crisis. He was so patient that often he didn't even think there really was a crisis.

Not only Kermit but others among Jimmy's friends noticed how fascinated Jimmy seemed to be with entertainment. Actually all of them loved it. And there was precious little of it in Leland or Stoneville. But on Saturday afternoons, the boys spent seven cents apiece, Kermit recalled the price, and went to the one movie theater in Leland. Jimmy never missed a Saturday. Kermit usually went with Jimmy, along with the other boys. Jimmy saw *The Wizard of Oz* and loved it. But he recalled being terrified when he was very young of the MGM lion. The boys also saw Westerns and serials such as *The Green Hornet* and *The Phantom.*

Gordon Jones loved the serial called *The Desert Hawk,* starring actor Gilbert Roland. In it, Roland, who had a mustache and a very dark, mysterious, Latin look—played twins: one good, one bad. One had a birthmark—a star—on his wrist. Gordon liked that serial so much that Jim made something for Gordon. Jimmy took a cork, whittled it into the shape of a star, and burned it so that Gordon could use it to rub a little black star onto his wrist.

Kermit Scott always recalled a movie serial called *Captain America.* All these serials were shown around the country for Saturday matinees, and they especially appealed to children in the 1940s.

Jimmy also loved radio shows. On weekdays he would hurry home from school to hear some shows. And on weekends he waited eagerly for the late afternoons, when a variety of wonderful shows came on. One was *The Shadow,* which was broadcast on Sunday afternoons, starring Lamont Cranston as the leading character— The Shadow himself. Only the audience—but none of the other people in the show—knew that Lamont Cranston and The Shadow were one and the same crime-fighting person. The show started with an announcer saying, "Who knows what evil lurks in the hearts of men? The Shadow knows." And then he let out a peal of deep-throated, eerie laughter. Jimmy loved the show and its suspense and mystery. Like children everywhere, he fell quiet to listen to that show for a fascinating half hour.

And Jimmy also loved the comedy shows on the radio. He especially liked Edgar Bergen, the ventriloquist, and his dummies, Charlie McCarthy and Mortimer Snerd. Charlie was quick-witted and fresh, and Mortimer was a silly and dull-witted country bumpkin. Sometimes grandmother Dear listened to the shows with Jimmy and enjoyed them, too. Mostly she

enjoyed how much Jimmy liked them. They talked about how much fun they were. Dear encouraged Jimmy, telling him she knew he was going to have a bright future and good luck, and she gave him self-confidence about his ideas and abilities.

Along with drawing birds and animals and collecting frogs and turtles, the movies and the radio shows counted as Jimmy's most favored pastimes.

Church

With Kermit Scott, and with his own family, Jimmy sometimes went to the Methodist church, an old Spanish-style stucco building, in Leland. Jimmy's father was a Methodist. His mother, who was a Christian Scientist, didn't have a church of that denomination to attend. So she went to the Methodist church with the family. Jimmy also went to other churches with his friends, particularly to the Baptist and Presbyterian churches in Leland. Stoneville had no churches. The Hensons had to travel to Leland on Sundays if they wanted to go to church.

One of Royal Frazier's fondest memories of

Jimmy centered on a Presbyterian church contest. It had something to do with a Bible story. Jimmy won first prize, a bat and a ball, in that contest. Jimmy already had a bat. So he kept the ball and gave the bat to Royal, who didn't have one. Royal was very touched by Jimmy's thoughtfulness and generosity.

To Gordon Jones, a Baptist, who also went to the Presbyterian church in Leland, Jimmy confided that he had never taken medicine.

Gordon was very surprised. He said, "How come?"

Jimmy said, "My mother and I are Christian Scientists. We believe in spiritual healing."

Sandra Toler, a classmate of Jimmy's, also learned that Jim didn't take medicine. Years later, Sandra heard that Jim died from a viral infection. He didn't go to a doctor soon enough after he became ill. She wondered if it was because he wasn't used to doctors or medicine. But Sandra also knew that nobody went to doctors much in Leland. Every family had its own home remedies for illnesses.

Sandra thought that Jimmy was a very smart,

sharp kid. Royal Frazier did, too. Royal couldn't say exactly why he had that impression of Jimmy. Jimmy didn't get the top marks in the school. But Royal thought the questions they asked each other and the ideas they talked about revealed Jimmy as a smart kid. Sandra thought Jimmy was very good at writing, even though the kids didn't have much to do with writing in the fifth and sixth grades.

Sandra and Jimmy were "girlfriend" and "boyfriend" for a little while in the sixth grade. They didn't do anything but say "hi" to each other in the school corridors, but that was enough for them to be considered a couple in those days. Sandra and Jimmy had a crush on each other. She called him "James." Years later, when her children were enthralled by the Muppets, a group of hand puppets that starred in a very popular televison show for kids called *Sesame Street,* she didn't recognize the name "Jim Henson." It took her quite a few years to find out that Jim Henson was her old boyfriend "James."

Leaving Stoneville and Leland

Jimmy finished the sixth grade in Leland with his friends, and Paul finished a higher grade and was getting ready to go to high school. Life went on as usual for the boys. But suddenly, one day, their father came home from the laboratory and said for the second time, "We're going back to Washington again. And this time I think we'll be staying quite a while."

Paul Henson, Sr., was being transferred again to work at the Department of Agriculture center in Beltsville, Maryland. The family would live in Hyattsville again. Jim would get a second chance to see all the monuments in Washington. That excited him. He felt very sorry to be leaving his friends behind. He went to the creek with Paul and caught frogs. But instead of taking them home, Jimmy set them free. He took the frogs that he already kept as pets, carried them back to the creek, and watched them hop away.

When Gordon Jones came to the house to visit the next day, they went riding on their horse and pony. Jimmy asked Gordon, "Will you take my dog Toby?" It was a little black, tan, and white mongrel that was used to running free in the country. Jimmy wasn't going to take it up to Maryland and have to keep it locked up all day. Toby was used to a free existence. "I love Toby," he said, "but he'll be better off here with you. He won't get hit by a car. I know you'll keep him safe."

Gordon said, "Sure, I'd love to have Toby. But you have to come back and visit us. 'Cuz Toby will miss you."

"Okay, sure," Jimmy said. "I'll be very lonesome without all of you."

But after the Hensons moved to Hyattsville, Maryland, none of Jimmy's old friends heard from him again. He didn't write letters to Gordon, or Royal, or Kermit, or the Baggett boys, or Sandra Toler.

Early Work
with Puppets

When Jimmy's family relocated to Hyattsville, Maryland, in 1948, the Hensons still didn't own a television set. By that time, about a million people were watching television in the United States. Some people saw shows on their neighbors' television sets. It was a popular pastime on Tuesday nights for people to get together in the house of a neighbor who owned a television set and watch the *Texaco Star Theater* (later called the *Milton Berle Show*). Uncle Miltie (as he was

called), a former vaudeville comedian, had the most popular show on television.

He put on wonderfully silly skits. People threw cream pies in each other's faces. Uncle Miltie wore wild costumes and wigs. He wore outsized shoes and walked on his ankles. With a funny accent, he told his guest stars, "I'll kill you a million times," making it sound as if he were saying "kiwll" and "miwllion"; all over the country people started saying that line to each other. NBC, the network that broadcast his show, was so thrilled with his appeal that it signed a thirty-year contract that paid Unclie Miltie a million dollars a year, a lot of money in those days.

By 1950, Jimmy Henson had seen enough television to fall in love with it. In Baltimore, about twenty miles from his family's house, more people were watching television than listening to radio. For children, and for adults, too, in that era, television was magical. Most shows were presented live in the evenings. People who later would grow up with round-the-clock television on countless channels and international broadcasts of ongoing wars and other spectacular events could never imagine how fresh and exciting television appeared in its early years. Nearly everyone was fascinated. A typical cartoon of the era in popular magazines and newspapers showed a shack with an antenna on its roof. The antenna belonged to a television set. No matter how poor a family was, it somehow managed to afford a television set. A set, which carried only black-and-white pictures, cost at least a couple of hundred dollars, usually more. That was a great deal of money in those days so people usually bought them on installment plans, which meant paying a little bit every month until it was paid off.

Because Jimmy's parents still didn't own a television set, he badgered them all the time to buy one. They resisted; Jimmy persisted.

Betty Henson told him, "You're driving us crazy."

"But you have to get one! You have to!" Jim said. "I need it!"

"For what?" Betty demanded.

"For my future," he said. "I absolutely love television . . . I love the idea that what you see is taking place somewhere else. I want to work in television one day," he told his parents. He would later tell the same thing to an interviewer about his memory of badgering his parents into buying a set.

Finally, when Jimmy was thirteen years old and in the seventh grade, his parents gave in and bought one. Then, for half an hour every night at about dinnertime, Jimmy watched Burr Tillstrom's show, *Kukla, Fran and Ollie*, starring two hand puppets with a real woman named Fran Allison on television. He also loved another show, Bil and Cora Baird's *Life with Snarky Parker*, another puppet production including Heathcliffe, a horse. These shows made a big impression on Jimmy.

He also loved the comedians Ernie Kovacs with his cigar, mustache, and grimace, and the slightly loony Stan Freberg, and Homer and Jethro, and the zany bandleader Spike Jones with his slapstick antics. Other parts of the entertainment world had their charms for Jimmy, too. He loved the cartoon serials in the newspapers—Walt Kelly's *Pogo,* for one. But most of all, Jim loved television itself. The medium was the message, and the message for Jimmy was: Get a job in television.

When he was sixteen, he looked for a job at all the little studios in Washington, D.C. He didn't find anything then. But he kept up his interest in performing by taking part in school plays in high school. They had nothing to do with puppets. He also became involved in a puppetry club. Then, in 1954, just after he graduated from Northwestern High School, he did get his foot in the door at a local station, WTOP. It needed some puppeteers for a Saturday morning program called *Junior Good Morning Show.* The pay was only ten dollars a day. Students were willing to work for that amount. Other people couldn't afford to. So Jimmy, the student, got the job. It was probably around that time that everyone started to call him Jim. He was growing up, and he was becoming very tall, just as he had hoped.

He asked a buddy from school, a boy named Russell Wall, to help him. Together the teenagers built some puppets. One was Pierre the French Rat. Others were cowboy puppets named Longhorn and Shorthorn. The boys took the puppets to WTOP for an audition and got the job.

That show lasted only a few weeks. But it did earn some good reviews in local newspapers. So Jim took the reviews and his puppets to NBC-TV, which put him on some little local shows on its owned-and-operated station WRC-TV. Jim enjoyed the work.

His father was puzzled and asked Jim, "Why are you so interested in working with puppets?"

"I'm not really in love with puppets," Jim answered. "But they give me a chance to work in television."

Paul Henson nodded and tried to get used to the idea. "You know you'll be much more secure with a job in the sciences," he told Jim.

"Television seems like a kind of novelty."

"But I want to work in televison, Dad," Jim insisted.

"But with puppets?" Paul Henson asked. "You should do something more practical."

Jim said nothing. He didn't know yet that puppets would allow him to combine all his talents—even some of his expertise at technical matters and building things—his affection for drawing, storytelling, and his respect for birds and all animals.

Paul Henson, Sr.'s old friend from Stoneville, Buford Willamson, had to travel from Mississippi to attend a Department of Agriculture meeting in Washington, D.C. So he visited the Hensons in their Hyattsville house.

Paul Henson, Sr., said of his son Paul, "He's doing real well in school." Paul, Jr., was excelling in the sciences. He could study to be an engineer. He had many interests, and a lot of fields would be open for him. "But I'm not sure about Jimmy," the father added.

Later on, Buford would laugh at the memory after little Jimmy Henson became known as Jim Henson, a world-famous puppeteer who coined the word "Muppets" for his prizewinning puppets. "It turned out real good, but at that time, the father was worried about him," Buford Williamson would reminisce.

Jim Gets His Own Television Show

Jim began attending college at the University of Maryland at the end of 1954, where he studied commercial art and theater arts. He was considering a career as a commercial artist. Some of his drawings from this time show he had a wonderful imagination, ability with color, and a talent for creating fantasy scenes with surprising details. For example, he drew a man atop a ladder that looked as if it leaned against a tipped-over tree. The man stretched his arms out. He

seemed to be reaching toward the faces of people suspended in the clouds. They had no bodies, and the faces were simple, with dots for eyes and lines for mouths and a few tufts of blond hair. Even with so few details, Jim could suggest so much. He painted many fanciful scenes. One was of a jazz band; green and blue blobs suggested some of the musicians. Others Jim drew in a more realistic way. The musicians played a little pink- and purple-colored guitar, bass and drums, and an orange-colored trombone. So full of fun, his work suggested his eventual designs for Muppets—a combination of marionettes and foam-rubber hand puppets—and their simple but very creatively conceived designs.

At the same time, outside of school, he found a job producing a five-minute puppet show called "Inga's Angle." It was part of a show called *Afternoon* on WRC, the station in Washington that NBC-TV owned and operated. That was a big victory for Jim. He was moving up, if only in one city. However, it was an important city with very influential people watching television there all the time.

Once again he needed the help of a friend to make the show work. So he asked his new girlfriend, Jane Nebel, a pretty girl who was a gifted ceramist and an art major at the university. Jane helped Jim operate the puppets. Jim and Jane put on their five-minute show for children late in the afternoon at 6:25 P.M. People saw it just before they watched the *Huntley-Brinkley Report,* a prestigious, prime-time news show. Jim and Jane put the show on again at 11:25 P.M., just before the popular *Tonight Show* hosted by the multitalented comedian and musician Steve Allen.

Their show made its debut on the air on May 9, 1955. Jane was thrilled with the positioning of the show. It appeared at times when very big audiences were tuned in. So many people saw it!

Jane said to Jim, "How did that happen? What luck! It couldn't be better."

Jim, who was a very quiet man, not given to

bursts of exuberance or excitement, said something like, "Hmmm. Seems that way." For Jim, the "hmmmm" was an all-purpose word. He used it a lot.

Soon the show developed a following. The "Inga's Angle" segment of *Afternoon* went through a name change to *Sam and Friends*. The show became a cult hit in Washington. Sam, one of Jim's Muppets, had a big bulb of a nose, and ears that stuck out, and a goofy expression of wild surprise in his huge eyes. Audiences loved him. He started Jim on the road to fame and fortune. Jim bought a white Thunderbird convertible with whitewall tires and a spare tire encased in white steel on the trunk. The show would continue on the air for another six years, until December 1961.

A great deal happened to Jim that helped him hone his skills with puppets during those years. His creative imagination developed constantly as he learned every aspect of the puppetry and television business. He worked as the inventor of puppets and as the show's director and set designer. He not only built his Muppets, as he already called them, but he performed with them. And he conducted the business management of his show.

Jim also learned how to manipulate television cameras and their varied lenses to create all kinds of visual effects. He and Jane rehearsed with their Muppets while watching themselves on a television monitor. It wasn't easy for them to work that way. For instance, when they moved to the right, their on-screen images moved to the left and vice-versa. But they forced themselves to rehearse that way because they wanted to see themselves the way that audiences would actually see them.

Also, in other puppet shows, the puppets did their skits on little stages that audiences could plainly see. Jim discarded that traditional stage— the old, historic, ministage of the Punch and Judy show used at carnivals. The television screen itself became Jim's stage. The change was subtle, but the idea was revolutionary. The puppets could do anything they pleased and go wherever they wanted, just as any characters in any story in the world did. Only the television screen gave them their boundaries.

While doing the television show, Jim also began a business creating silk-screen posters for college events. His silk-screening business became so successful that it took up all his time. He was having a hard time fitting his college classes into his schedule along with the television show. Jane noticed how much time the silk-screen business took up. She told him he was trying to do too much. He might have to cut out at least one thing. As usual, all Jim said was, "Mmmmmmmm."

But then one night at dinner, in a little Italian restaurant that they loved, with a red-checkered tablecloth, and brilliant Chianti wine, and tasty meatballs and spaghetti, he confided in Jane. By then she was both his best friend and his girlfriend. He said, "I've been thinking over my goals. I've decided what I'm going to concentrate on, what makes me truly happy. So I'm going to concentrate on building a career in television. That's what I've always wanted to do."

"Then that's what I think you should do, Jim," she said. "You can always go back to silk screening or any kind of artwork you want, if you change your mind."

So he didn't spend less time working. But he spent more time performing with his Muppets at WRC-TV, the NBC-owned-and-operated station in Washington, D.C. All his creativity went into that. The show became so popular that it won a local Emmy. For Jim, life was just beginning to take shape.

But in April 1956, he and his family suffered a catastrophe. Jim's brother, Paul, was killed in an automobile accident. The shock was unbearable for the family. Although their interests had been different, Paul and Jim had been very close, loving, and proud of each other's talents. Jim felt the loss deeply. Some people thought that he decided to work harder than ever after Paul's death—as though he were living for two.

That year, Jim created Kermit the Frog. Well, Kermit wasn't exactly a frog yet, but he could easily develop in that direction. He was a green creature, which Jim fashioned out of an old green coat that had belonged to his mother. Jim also cut a Ping-Pong ball in half and used the halves for Kermit's eyes. Kermit, the green creature, was a hand puppet—a Muppet. Above all, Jim wanted all his Muppets to be flexible. He wanted them to respond to a puppeteer's flexible hand for subtle movements and expressions.

As time went on, the collection of Muppets that Jim and his colleagues developed would become varied. Jim would hire many creative people to help him. Some Muppets would be very complex in construction and include electronics. But Kermit was a classic Muppet: a combined hand-and-rod puppet. The puppeteer placed one hand inside Kermit's head and controlled its movements by pivoting the hand from the wrist and operating the mouth with the fingers and thumbs. Then the puppeteer could use his other hand to operate two almost invisible rods that controlled the puppet's hands. Sometimes two puppeteers worked on the same puppet.

Jane Nebel still worked closely with Jim all the time. They had no live sound on the show *Sam and Friends*. But they made the Muppets lip-synch songs done by prominent pop musicians of the era. One tune was "That Old Black Magic," sung by the gravelly voiced trumpeter Louis Prima and his wife, Keely Smith. Prima copied the great jazz trumpeter and singer Louis Armstrong. For that skit, Kermit wore a short dark wig. Jane would also recall how she and Jim used a recording of "Banana Boat," a novelty tune sung by the comedian Stan Freberg. Puppet Sam was Kermit's opposite—a very excitable character.

Jane thought the appeal of the show resided in its qualities of "abandon" and "nonsense," she would reflect years later. It was all "somewhat experimental," she said. She watched Jim develop a fantastic-looking cast of characters for their Muppet group for *Sam and Friends*. Aside from Kermit and Sam, along came Professor Madcliffe, with a ring of bushy hair encircling his head. The ring joined his mustache to his hair in an unbroken line. Jim created plain, brown Harry with white pince-nez glasses; and Hank with a huge mouth like a horse's and a blond wig; and Omar with a little nose and wide mouth; and Yorick, a bright blue Muppet with an overhanging brow that made him resemble Neanderthal man. There were shmoo-like Wilkins; and Wontkins, who looked like a mushroom; and yellow Mushmellon, who resembles a flying saucer; and Moldy Hay; and Scoop; and Icky Gunk; and Henrietta—weird and wonderful creatures with only the loosest connection in their appearance to the animal world.

In those days, Jim did nearly everything by

himself. He not only designed and built the Muppets—he also wrote their skits. He constructed their props and backgrounds and the opening titles for the show. Jane helped him perform and put the Muppets through their paces. Jim constantly went into the control room to learn lessons from the technicians. As time went on, Jim began writing sketches that required him to use his own voice on television. At first he was shy about doing that.

In 1957, he and Jane Nebel formed a legal partnership for their work in puppetry. Their Muppets had begun to star in TV commercials. The television ads brought them a degree of fame and a significant new source of income. They did their first commercial for Wilkins Coffee; they would make more than three hundred commercials for Wilkins Coffee alone. Two of Jim's Muppet characters starred in the commercials: Wilkins, who drank the coffee, and Wontkins, who wouldn't drink it. Wilkins won out in competitions and tussles with Wontkins. In one commercial, Wilkins blew Wontkins to pieces. The commercials lasted only seven seconds, but they made a lasting impression on audiences. The commercials were humorous at a time when most television ads were very serious. Only a few other advertisers turned away from heaping forcefully delivered, lavish praise on products and turned to humor as a way of presenting them. Jim's wit caught on with other sponsors. He was asked to do commercials for Royal Crown Cola, Purina Dog Chow, Ivory Snow, and IBM, to mention a few of his clients. Big accounts!

The Muppets commercials gave Jim a chance and a reason to develop a cast of characters. Rowlf the Dog came to life for a Purina Dog Chow commercial. Another was a monster that ate a computer and became the basis for Cookie Monster; he would become famous on *Sesame Street,* a phenomenally successful educational show for children that would change Jim's life just as it influenced generations of young children.

For yet another commercial, the first full-sized

Muppet, the La Choy Dragon, had a person inside his costume. This Muppet prepared the way for the creation of Big Bird, who would become one of *Sesame Street*'s most popular characters. The dragon was especially effective for color television, with his orangy-yellow skin and purple-, pink-, orange-, and yellow-colored patches all over his body. And technical tricks let its mouth breathe fire! That was spectacular. Color television was becoming popular, even though color television sets were much more expensive than black-and-white ones. Jim saw the handwriting on the wall about the allure of color television.

Like most television shows of the era, *Sam and Friends* was broadcast live from a studio. But advertisers produced commercials on film. They gave Jim a chance to learn about working with film.

He could have rested on his laurels and done only commercials to earn his living. For the most part, with his Muppets, he did commercials and guest appearances on other people's television shows, plus his own show *Sam and Friends,* for which he won a local Emmy.

But Jim decided he wanted to study the history of puppets more. He wanted to do his job as perfectly and as knowledgeably as possible. So he asked an old school friend, Bob Payne, to work with Jane on the show *Sam and Friends.* Then Jim went to Europe to study old-fashioned, traditional puppetry techniques and history.

He was so impressed with what he saw that when he came home and rejoined *Sam and Friends,* he tried to produce a traditional, complex version of the classic fairy tale "Hansel and Gretel" for a live audience for *Sam and Friends.* But the skit failed. Jim realized that he would have to give up on that type of overcomplicated drama with puppets. It was good for classic, European puppet theater, but not for the young, dynamic, less formal art of puppetry for American television audiences.

Through trial, error, and hard work, Jim was developing his Muppets appropriately to fit in with the thriving American television industry. He kept exploring and experimenting. Jim was taking everything in life more seriously than ever after his brother's death. And Jim and Jane's personal relationship had developed more, too.

The reputation of the charming Muppets spread. They were often invited to perform on network television programs such as *The Tonight Show* and the *Today* show. Jim was still struggling to establish his Muppets as a very profitable, regular part of the entertainment industry. But he was enjoying himself and making progress, endearing the Muppets to audiences.

In 1959, Jim and Jane, having become very sure of their love for each other, finally decided to get married. Jim now had a beard and long hair. His mother begged him to cut his hair and shave off the beard. Jim did it to please her. Jane hadn't asked him to do anything of the sort.

But 1959 was the last year of the term of the conservative Republican President of the United States, General Dwight D. Eisenhower. Jim's mother had a rather conservative lifestyle. Jim and his beard heralded a more modern, liberal period—first the beatnik, then the hippie era—that respected or at least accepted creative people and their individualistic tastes and lifestyles. "Do your own thing" became the new rule for society. The more liberal era would begin in 1960, when the country elected young, glamorous President John F. Kennedy. His political views and speeches inspired a fresh outlook and optimism for the country's young people. And President Kennedy's fashionable wife, Jacqueline, loved and encouraged the arts.

Jim Henson, not really wanting to part with his beard in the last days of the conservative 1950s, nevertheless did it. He sent the shaved-off beard to Jane as a wedding present and wrote a note saying, "From Samson to Delilah."

For the wedding ceremony, Jim wore a suit with a flower in his lapel. Jane wore a traditional long, white gown with a modest scoop neck, a bouffant skirt, and a train. In their wedding picture they looked happy, comfortable, and relaxed with each other.

Finally, six years after he started college, Jim finished his senior year and got his degree. He hadn't been able to keep up a full load of courses to finish in four years because he had been too busy with his Muppets and television. For his graduation he and Jane drove to the ceremonies in a second-hand Rolls-Royce Silver Cloud with a sunroof, a symbol of his early success.

Jim remained a very quiet man who spoke in an exceptionally soft, relaxed voice. But inside Jim lived a dashing showman. Driving his attention-getting cars, he might sometimes wear a black top hat. That flamboyant, whimsical instinct in Jim showed itself off in his Muppets and his cars— and perhaps in the beard that he had loved and would eventually grow back. He had already owned a white Thunderbird and a Porsche Speedster, both convertibles, before he graduated from college.

Both the Henson Family and the Muppet Business Grow

Soon after they married, Jane became pregnant with their daughter Lisa. Born in 1960, Lisa was only two months old when Jim and Jane took her with them in their Rolls-Royce to Detroit, to the Puppeteers of America annual convention. There Jim began to meet many of his idols. Some were well-known stars in the world of puppetry and entertainment. They became his friends.

One was Burr Tillstrom, who drove Jim to a

busy section of downtown Detroit and opened the car's sunroof. Jim stuck Kermit out of the roof and performed with him. Jane would later reflect on what a big impression she thought the Hensons made at the convention.

Two of the people they met were puppeteers Mike and Frances Oznowicz. The next year at the Puppeteers of America convention, in California, they introduced the Hensons to their teenage son, Frank Oz. Jim loved the way Frank performed with puppets. Frank was a wizard with them. And Jim immediately wanted to hire Frank as a replacement for Jane, who had become pregnant with their second child, daughter Cheryl. Jane announced it was time for her to retire from performing. But Frank Oz couldn't leave school to replace Jane. So Jim hired another talented puppeteer, Jerry Juhl, who worked at a California station. Jerry joined Jim on *Sam and Friends* for its last season in Washington, D.C.

Then Jim, who was twenty-six years old, kept concentrating on the commercials and guest

appearances with the Muppets on major network television shows. The Hensons visited New York City so often for work, looking for new work, and making pilot shows with the hope of a happy landing on network television, that they decided to move to Manhattan in 1962. Their friend Burr Tillstrom helped them find an apartment in the building where he lived on fashionable Beekman Place. Jane became pregnant again, this time with the Hensons' son Brian, born in 1963. By 1965, she would have another son, John. In 1964, it was clear that the Hensons needed more space as well as peace and quiet for their brood.

They moved to Greenwich, Connecticut, in January 1964, and kept the Muppets business headquarters in a building on East 53rd Street in another posh Upper East Side neighborhood of New York City. It consisted of only two rooms with a bathroom, but it sufficed for a while for Jim's staff: a secretary; Jerry Juhl; and Don Sahlin, an experienced puppet designer and builder.

When Don joined the staff, he created Rowlf the Dog. That Muppet required two puppeteers to operate for a Purina Dog Chow commercial in 1963. Don had a wild sense of humor and built all sorts of contraptions to make the workshop-office an exciting place. He set off little explosions sometimes. He put white mice in an aquarium to live together. One puppeteer noticed how the mice all slept together. "It was beautiful to watch," said that puppeteer. Don also devised a kind of tube that the mice ran through, circulating it throughout the office—over chandeliers and across desks.

Next, Frank Oz, just out of high school, joined the staff to help with performing. His arrival freed Jerry Juhl to do more writing. Frank Oz performed with Rowlf the Dog on *The Jimmy Dean Show* from 1963 to 1966. Jim actually operated Rowlf along with Oz's help. Oz controlled Rowlf's paws so that the doggie could play the piano while Jim operated the head. And Jim sang a little and exchanged chitchat with

Jimmy Dean on every show. This was the first time that Jim interacted, through his Muppets, with a live character. *The Jimmy Dean Show* staff coached Henson, particularly in the art of delivering punch lines for jokes.

Frank Oz would recall his entry into the world of the Muppets in August 1963, when he was nineteen years old:

> I walked up those narrow stairs and opened the door to the Muppets studio . . . Don Sahlin worked in the back workshop next to Jim's animation stand and opposite the big Yorick head . . . Jerry Juhl had a desk in the front room . . . Opposite Jerry's desk there was a dart board on the closet door with lots and lots of holes on the door. Above the dart board hung the papier-mâché moose head that would light up. There was a big black chair and ottoman. Jim's chair. He would sit on it or lie in it, working on character or script ideas.

This is the room where Jim, wearing his bright flowered ties and speaking just above a whisper, would hold meetings with clients.

In his office, Don Sahlin rigged up his practical jokes, and the whole staff learned about the assassination of President John F. Kennedy, and ate sandwiches with dill pickles that Frank Oz, fresh from California, had never tasted before. "Everything here was new and strange and exciting and adult," he recalled.

At around this time, Jim became interested in filmmaking. He didn't earn much money with his experimental filmmaking. Basically it consisted of animation that he created by making a drawing, filming it, then developing the drawing until he had an animated film project. He loved doing it. His activities with the Muppets paid the bills while Jim branched off into experimental films. His first big work was called *Timepiece,* a fable about a man caught up in the trap of time.

The clock enslaved him. The idea was actually more complicated than that. Jim created many concepts relating to time—musical time, philosophical time, and more—for the film.

Jim even played a part in *Timepiece*. He stood on a diving board and jumped off it into the pool. He did it while he was wearing a formal suit. Just as he was about to jump, he realized he was terrified. But he didn't let his fear stop him.

His wife knew that Jim never would have jumped off that high diving board if it had been just for fun. But it was for work. He would do anything for work. He was spending more and more time in New York City with his work.

He made two more experimental films in the 1960s, *Youth '68* and *The Cube*. But first came his success with his side venture, *Timepiece*. Filled with bizarre images and events, the movie was given a showing at the Museum of Modern Art in May 1965. Then it ran for eighteen months at a Manhattan theater and received a nomination for an Academy Award! *Timepiece* didn't

win the Oscar, but it was a brave new venture. Jim later produced other experimental movies.

Jim said he "just loved what one could do with the montaging of visual images." He also was experimentng with stream of conscious-ness—the quick flow from one idea to another, with the images themselves as the banks of the river of his imagination. For him, the images and the music were the main point.

At the same time, he kept taking his lively cast of Muppets onto renowned television shows: *The Jack Paar Show*, for one, and *The Ed Sullivan Show*, probably the most popular variety show on television at the time. Jim went to *The Ed Sullivan Show* with Kermit the Creature. He still wasn't exactly a frog, because his feet had no flippers yet. For the debut of the Muppets on *The Ed Sullivan Show*, Ed Sullivan mistakenly called them "pup-pets." And he made another big mistake: Jim's name came out as Jim Newsome. But Jim didn't take offense. Ed Sullivan invited them back many times, and finally got their names right.

Rowlf the Dog had received tons of fan mail for his appearances on *The Jimmy Dean Show*. But Jim couldn't develop the characters of his Muppets more, because nobody was offering them a show of their own. Jim did get a chance to do a pilot show in 1965 at the invitation of Jon Stone and Tom Whedon, young writers who loved the charm and whimsy of the Muppets. The writers hoped to tell the story of Cinderella, the fairy-tale princess, over a period of months for ABC-TV. But ABC didn't buy the show.

However, Jim managed to bring the idea to life a few years later. The original writers, Stone and Whedon, changed the story, with music by a young Fall River, Massachusetts-born composer, Joe Raposo, who would eventually work on *Sesame Street*. A takeoff on the Cinderella story, combining real actors and Muppets, the show was produced in Toronto, Canada. ABC broadcast it in 1970, with great success in the United States. It was the most ambitious Muppet production up till then.

Kermit's personality became more developed as Cinderella's subtly philosophical coachman. Jim Henson directed that show, called *Hey Cinderella*. It led to two more Muppet fairy tales: *The Frog Prince* and *The Muppet Musicians of Bremen*. Kermit got to play a real frog in *The Frog Prince*. And a quartet of barnyard animals triumphed over evil and played Dixieland music in *The Muppet Musicians of Bremen*. In Jim's project, Bremen, which was actually a city in Germany, became transferred to a city in Louisiana, the home of Dixieland (or early New Orleans jazz music).

These fairy tales still didn't constitute a regular television show for Jim's Muppets. The way was open for him to go back to making experimental films for adults. That's what he wanted to do. But something had already happened that would bring him fame and fortune beyond his wildest dreams. It was a show that would not only change his life—it changed the lives of millions of children and adults around the world.

The Muppets Find a Home on *Sesame Street*

In 1966, the Carnegie Institute wanted to reach out and use television to help poor and culturally deprived children to learn to cope with school and modern society. So the Carnegie Institute decided to start a study of the programs for children on television. Joan Ganz Cooney, a producer at WNET, the public television channel in New York City, accepted the

113

invitation to head the study. She had a bachelor's degree in education, though she didn't teach school. Through research, she discovered that children's television programs were a kind of wasteland. She recommended that public television supply more nourishing fare.

By 1968, her project was raising funds for research and production, and the Children's Television Workshop was established. Among the three producers Mrs. Cooney hired was Jon Stone. He had already become experienced in working with Jim Henson and the Muppets for the Cinderella programs. As the Children's Television Workshop began to take shape, it held seminars in Boston. Experts on education went there to air their views.

Mrs. Cooney had already become aware of Jim Henson through his commercials. She thought they were very funny, but she hadn't even considered the Muppets or Jim Henson for her new project. Jon Stone mentioned the Muppets. He thought she should include them in the show.

At one of the seminars, a tall, very erect man, with brownish hair, showed up and sat down in the back of the room. He was dressed in a bohemian style, in a T-shirt, jeans, a jean jacket, and loafers—his usual outfit. And he had a hippie-style beard. Mrs. Cooney worried about his appearance. She thought he was a hippie or possibly a terrorist of some kind. It was an era when groups as extreme as the Weathermen were actually involved in bombings. Mrs. Cooney whispered to Dave Connell, one of the producers she had hired, Dave Connell, that she was afraid the newcomer might harm the people at the seminar.

"It isn't very likely," Dave Connell said. "That's Jim Henson."

Mrs. Cooney began to talk to her staff and Jim Henson. Jon Stone said that if Mrs. Cooney didn't use Jim Henson's Muppets, she should forget about using puppets at all. They were the best. At first Jim wanted to keep making experimental, fantasy films for adults. But he thought it over and decided to go ahead with the children's program. He knew it would give him a chance to work with puppets and animation. He would also be able to reach children's minds. From his experiences with his own kids, he knew children could be a sophisticated, intelligent audience. Soon Jim was working with the show's producers and a staff of about a dozen creative people, including Joe Raposo, who became the musical director.

The pilot show became ready for taping in July 1969. But the show still didn't have a name. Staffers proposed all sorts of silly or boring names. Nobody liked them. Then somebody said, "'Sesame Street.'" Nobody really like that name, either. The show's staffers figured that kids would never catch on to the connection between the name of the show and the line from the old fairy tale "Open Sesame!" Those were the magic words that opened up a treasure cave, and were first used in "The Arabian Nights." But when it came time to vote on the show's name, people voted for *Sesame Street*.

Rehearsed and filmed at the Reeves Studio on West 83rd Street and Broadway, *Sesame Street* quickly became an important and famous show for children. Mrs. Cooney realized that kids loved television commercials. They were fast, slick, often funny, and to the point. They had tunes and slogans that stuck in kids' minds. Mrs. Cooney decided to use sixty-second skits to teach kids to count and spell, or at least to learn the alphabet, and to understand concepts. Instead of product sponsors, numbers and letters would bring kids each show. For example, the letters M and N and the number 8 could sponsor a show. And so they did. The idea appealed to children.

Furthermore, the show combined live actors and Muppets as its cast of characters. For the live actors, *Sesame Street* decided upon employing men and women of all races. That way, no one sex or ethnic or racial group would seem to be in control or in charge.

Jim Henson produced wonderful skits that

taught numbers to preschool children. But most important of all were the Muppet characters, who caught the fancy of children and kept them coming back day after day to see the shows with new lessons and their favorite Muppets—among them, Big Bird, Oscar the Grouch, Ernie and Bert, Cookie Monster, Elmo, Kermit, and many more.

Cookie Monster evolved from the old monster Jim had used for *Sam and Friends*. Kids loved him. They also adored Big Bird, a six-year-old, eight foot, two inch tall, yellow-feathered vision with red legs and a smiley, sweet expression. All Big Bird's hundreds of yellow feathers were sewn on by hand. Big Bird had to have ideas explained to him countless times, until he finally caught on. That was the way children learned, too.

Jim hired Big Bird's builder, Kermit Love, because Jim and Kermit had had such great rapport when they met for a lunch date. (The name Kermit must have appealed to Jim, too. How many times in life does a person meet a likable person with the name Kermit? This was Jim's *second* friend named Kermit.) First, Jim asked Kermit Love to work on the La Choy Dragon, a character already developed. Then Jim wanted Kermit to work on "other things," Kermit remembered Jim saying. So Kermit built Big Bird's body, guided by Jim's conception. Designer Don Sahlin added the head for the bird.

Kermit would later explain that he kept the image of Jim Henson himself in mind for Big Bird. "[Jim] was well over six feet tall—and that loping gait he had when he walked down a hallway" was the same loping gait that T. Kermit Scott, Jim's childhood friend, had noticed.

Details for the show and for the animals seemed endless. First of all, Jim Henson received guidelines for each show from the Children's Television Workshop panel of educational advisers. They knew the ideas they wanted to put into each show. But sometimes the panel presented them in a very boring way. Jim had to bring them to life. He and the staff improvised

119

and used jokes and visual gags and funny expressions on the Muppets' faces, or tricks for their movements to make humorous points and entertain the children. Jim soon found himself heart and soul in love with and committed to *Sesame Street*.

As he explained, "I put aside a few other areas I'd been working on, because at that point it was as if the audience wanted *Sesame Street* and it was what I should be putting my time and energy into. Since the beginning, the Muppets have had a sort of life of their own and we—the people who work with them—serve that life, and the audience, and the characters. It's something I don't particularly dictate at all."

Creative artists often explain their motives for working in this way. They feel that their inspiration comes from a higher source and takes possession of their spirit. The creative artist isn't really the boss; he or she is simply a vessel for communicating.

But Jim Henson actually did take charge of

the Muppets. The live actors who played in the show with the Muppets did their rehearsing and shooting of the script on Mondays through Thursdays. Their parts were then connected with the Muppets. Henson did that sort of work with his Muppets on Fridays at the studio.

"Henson was a very quiet, mellow, laid-back kind of guy," recalled actor Harold Miller, who played a character named Gordon on the show in 1973 and 1974. "All the personal inventions," the ideas for the skits, "they were Henson's personal little inventions. And he didn't make big money doing this work." The big money came a few years later when he started to do *The Muppet Show* and films in London.

Sesame Street made its debut on November 10, 1969. One of its most prominent characters was Kermit the Frog, now definitely a frog complete with flippers. He had a liking for dressing up in costumes. With his trench coat, Kermit cut quite a figure as a roving reporter. That role he loved.

122

Other characters who started with the show were Bert and Ernie—Bert, a serious type prone to worrying, and Ernie, a careless, dreamy fellow with a poetic soul. As roommates, they kept fighting and making up. No matter what their differences, they remained best friends and helped each other.

Then there was the bright blue Cookie Monster with his wide mouth, who charmed everyone. When offered his choice between a trip to Hawaii and a cookie, he took the cookie. Cookie Monster became a classic Muppet. Oscar the Grouch, who lived in a garbage can, was another popular character. And Count Von Count, with his pointy ears, looked like Dracula. But he committed his entire being to teaching numbers with a chorus of enthusiastic little Muppets. One Muppet enchanted audiences with such interludes as his fantasy of visiting the moon and his even greater desire to come back to Earth and sleep in his own bed. And there were Guy Smiley and Grover, and even, as time went on, Muppets who made only one appearance in their whole lives. One such Muppet was a talking lettuce.

The Muppet workshop was a magical place to see. It brimmed over with creations. Dolls and bits of dolls and material were strewn every place. The workshop kept needing larger quarters, so they moved from East 53rd to East 67th Street.

Harold Miller was a classical actor who had appeared in the winter touring company of the New York Shakespeare Festival and the Shakespeare Festival in Stratford, Connecticut. He thought he was an unlikely guy to join *Sesame Street*. But he received an invitation to audition, and his agent urged him to do it in 1972. By that time, *Sesame Street* was a tremendous hit. So he said yes.

"It was kind of a cute little script," Harold said about the audition script. "My name in the show was Gordon. The script was about a confrontation between myself and the woman who would play my wife on the show. She had gone shopping, and I came home and said, 'There's no dinner.' And we went on and on. But we decided: let's not fight. We'll go out and eat. That was our scene."

Harold didn't hear from the producers of *Sesame Street* for three or four months. "I thought I didn't have the part. But they had been sending the tape around the country to see who the kids and educational experts wanted as the next Gordon. So they wanted me," he said.

Jon Stone, the executive producer, took Harold to dinner and asked what ideas he would bring to the show.

Harold said, "I want to appeal not just to children but to adults, too."

That made the executive producer very happy.

"And instead of namby pamby stuff," Harold reminisced about the way the show was created, "I wanted to say, 'Hey man, what's happening?' A production staffer said I couldn't say it. People wouldn't understand what I was talking about, he said. And I said, "Yes, we have to broaden their [horizons].' He allowed me to do it and encouraged me to stay on the show.

"There were other good people on the show: Will Lee, Sonya Manzano, Emilio Delgado, Northern Calloway, Bob McGrath, Loretta Long who played my wife—all actors with a knack for interacting with Muppets."

It was a very good time to be part of *Sesame Street*. The show was well established. A study proved that it reached middle-class children. They may not have been the original inspiration and target audience for the show, but they made it a big hit. There was a cast album made, including the poignant song "It's Not Easy Bein' Green." Joe Raposo had written it for Kermit the Frog. Kermit would croon its lyrics about such sad situations as being overlooked because of his color. He sang the song many times. Once he sang it to Ray Charles, the great soul singer. Ray joined in and supplied his throbbing lift to the music. "It's Not Easy Bein' Green" became beloved by adults. "Rubber Duckie," a song by another talented composer with the show, Jeff Moss, became an international hit, too, popular with children.

Harold Miller was on the cast album, which was put out by CBS Records. And Harold had the pleasure of watching the staff invent and introduce a new Muppet, an elephant named Snuffleupagus.

The cast, which worked hard, was well rewarded. "I taped two shows a day, four days a week, with weekends off," Harold recalled. He received his scripts on Fridays, and when he went to work on Mondays, he sometimes discovered the producers had thrown the script out, and they gave the cast a new one.

The actors did a lot of work in the studio and also flew to other cities to do live shows—to Atlanta, Georgia, and El Paso, Texas, and New Mexico, and Mexico. The Muppets, of course, went, too. Harold had some happy memories of those days. It was a great spectacle to watch Big Bird getting carried onto planes, with his hundreds of feathers sewn on by hand by Big Bird's creators. Kermit Love traveled with Big Bird, too.

Harold was particularly enchanted by the effect *Sesame Street* had on his career. Suddenly everyone recognized him. "I'd get stopped on the street by kids and their mothers. 'There's Gordon! There's Gordon!' They asked for my autograph."

Harold saw Jim Henson on Fridays, when he came to the studio to work with the Muppets. "Henson was withdrawn, not gregarious, quiet, understated. I never saw him dressed in a suit or tie. He had a beard," said Harold. Among all the staffers, Frank Oz was Jim's main man, his closest associate.

The kids of the staffers loved to go to the studio. Henson's kids were quite young then. In 1970, he and Jane had their youngest and last child, a daughter named Heather. The other Henson kids were old enough to visit Dad's workplace and see what he was doing. Jon Stone's four-year-old daughter went, too. Harold Miller had a daughter, Genie, who was eleven at that time and went to visit him. Genie brought along a girlfriend and proudly showed off that her dad acted on *Sesame Street*. Harold's son, Harold, Jr. often went to the set. Harold recalled, "Henson's kids looked at it all as if this was nothing unusual. This was his job."

When Henson talked to Harold, the subject was always the show. "His conversation always related to the Muppets." He wanted them to look perfectly real. "He spent hours and hours setting up the format for the Muppets, where they were positioned, the angles from which they speak to each other. Every now and then an actor's wrist or hand would show when he operated a Muppet. That was no good. It wasn't just enough to put your hand inside. You had to twist it in such ways. One little sequence could take hours. The work was especially obvious when Oscar popped out of his ash can. You knew something special was about to happen."

One actor-staffer, Caroll Spinney, provided the raspy voice of Oscar as well as the higher, more singsongy voice of Big Bird. The actor had a five-inch television monitor around his neck so he could see where he was going. For example, he could see himself moving to the left while everyone saw him going to the right.

Harold especially loved the camaraderie between the actors, producers, and writers. If they had problems, they sat down and hashed them out. The producers gave the actors room for improvisation. One day, Big Bird appeared. Harold was sitting with his shirt off. Big Bird splashed him with water. So they skipped the script. Harold said, "Big Bird, did you see what you did to me?" Big Bird started to say something, but Harold said, "Don't say a word." And this went on for a few minutes, Harold completely wet, and Big Bird's eyebrows completely down.

And some of the lessons taught by *Sesame Street* probed into deep matters. The Muppets taught children about big and mysterious concepts in life. When one of the human characters, Will Lee, who played Mr. Hooper, died, the show tried to explain his disappearance to children. The street's adults told Big Bird that Mr. Hooper had died. Big Bird had enjoyed a long relationship with Mr. Hooper and had always mispronounced Mr. Hooper's name, calling him "Looper" and "Dooper." Big Bird seemed to understand that Mr. Hooper was dead. But then Big Bird asked, "When will he be back?" Slowly he came to understand what had really happened. And so did children.

The show involved a lot of work, but it was fun for everyone. A staff psychologist analyzed the show to try to determine what children paid attention to. The producers did brainstorming. Harold had a good life while he worked on the show. He wore jeans and a work shirt—his usual costume. The salaries were excellent. Actors got two months' vacation with pay. *Sesame Street* got the royal treatment for its success. Harold met

Joan Ganz Cooney at a cast party at one of the most fashionable restaurants in New York City, Tavern on the Green, in Central Park. The Children's Television Workshop had business offices for the publicity, secretarial, and payroll people housed at glamorous One Lincoln Plaza, the ASCAP building, facing Lincoln Center.

In 1974, just before Harold Miller left the show, the producers took a segment of *Sesame Street* in which he appeared, and they put it in the Museum of Broadcasting, now called the Museum of Television and Radio. In this segment, Harold, as "Gordon," with Stevie Wonder, a great blind musician, singer, and composer, appeared, along with Big Bird.

Other segments had other celebrities; countless celebrities appeared happily on *Sesame Street*. The pretty blond actress and comedian Goldie Hawn kissed Kermit in one segment and turned into a Muppet; when she realized what had happened, she fainted. The incident, accomplished by a visual trick, with a Muppet made to look a bit like Goldie and substituted for her on-screen, gave Kermit the chance to show off his sense of humor. He commented wryly, calmly, and sensibly how some people weren't very good at withstanding shock.

Other celebrities, to name only a few people, were the beautiful actress Raquel Welch, folksinger Pete Seeger, actor Joe Pesci, and trumpeter Wynton Marsalis, who loved to teach children about music. Bebop jazz trumpeter Dizzy Gillespie came on the show dressed as a swami with a turban and sang "Swing Low, Sweet Cadillac," his own parody of the spiritual hymn "Swing Low, Sweet Chariot."

Harold felt that *Sesame Street* was one of the finest hours of his career, but he wanted to do other things. He went to California and costarred in a movie with a famous actor, Lloyd Bridges, then did many other interesting roles. Some of the same crew members Harold worked with on *Sesame Street* remained on the show for the rest of the century.

By the year 2000, *Sesame Street* has lasted thirty-one years and won more than fifty Emmys, some of them for Outstanding Children's Show.

Sesame Street Keeps Growing and Collecting Honors

The Henson kids especially liked to visit their father's workplace in New York during school holidays. Otherwise, the Henson kids lived a secluded life in an old farmhouse in Greenwich, Connecticut. The house came to resemble a Jim Henson workshop, since Jim worked all the time. The children liked to get involved in their own crafts projects, too.

Their closest neighbor was a man in his

nineties, who lived alone with an old, talking parrot. The Henson house was separated by a busy street from the rest of Greenwich. And Jim's arty appearance seemed to underscore the Hensons' differences from the other people who lived in Greenwich, Connecticut. Most of them were conservative-looking people with important jobs in large corporations. Jim let his hair and beard grow again.

One day, Cheryl had to go to a doctor. Discovering that her father listed his occupation as "puppeteer," the doctor commented that it was irresponsible for a puppeteer to have so many children. But that was before *Sesame Street* became a world-famous program!

Actually there was nothing irresponsible about Jim Henson. He was a very savvy businessman. He just liked to keep his appearance earthy and simple. Despite all the fame he would achieve, he remained humble and unassuming. He knew people liked him, of course. Even so, his friends still thought he was shy.

They had a theory that he wore a beard to cover up scars from a case of adolescent acne. He never raised his voice, never shouted at people, and if he disapproved of something, he would simply say, "Hmmmmmm."

He reportedly conducted business in a deceptively simple way, too. He worked out any complications or problems between Jim Henson Productions and the Children's Television Workshop in person at lunches with Joan Ganz Cooney. They didn't have to take along any lawyers.

Jim was completely wrapped up in his work, not his home life. In that way, he was quite different and not as down-to-earth as most people. He had a burning desire to produce a new show with the Muppets. He wanted to do it for adults, and he began discussing it with executives at ABC, then at CBS and NBC. Jim made two pilot shows produced by ABC in 1974 and 1975. But nobody wanted to take a chance. According to Brian Henson, the eldest son in the family, the show, which Jim called *The*

Muppet Show: Sex and Violence, was wacky and edgy: "It wasn't really about sex and violence. It was the Muppet version of sex and violence. But it made fun of television and advertising, and it was different from anything else that was on." The executives at the major American networks told Jim Henson that Muppets were strictly for children.

But a daring, rich, and visionary British producer named Sir Lew Grade saw one of the pilot shows. Lord Grade had his own very successful company in London. He decided to get involved in the project. Lord Grade and Jim Henson became partners. And Jim began spending a lot of time in London.

The Muppet Show was syndicated, beginning on September 26, 1976, to local stations in the United States and abroad. And it became a very successful show by the late seventies, "seen every week by two hundred and thirty-five million viewers in over a hundred countries," wrote David Owen in *The New Yorker* magazine.

In this period, a very important Muppet character developed. Miss Piggy had made her first appearance as one of many piggies in a show, *The Herb Alpert Special,* in the United States in 1974. That was the first year that the Macy's Thanksgiving Day Parade included a float with *Sesame Street* characters.

Miss Piggy soon emerged as a star in *The Muppet Show*—an actress with dreams and ambitions for a glamorous career that conflicted with her adoration of Kermit the Frog. She pursued both her career and Kermit constantly. The results were very funny.

One night she actually used a karate chop on Kermit. That inspired the show's creators to give Miss Piggy's character greater dimensions. At times she could become an unbridled battler, but always with her softly expressive eyes and their seductively long lashes.

She appeared in lavish costumes, wigs, and makeup. She even donned a black leather outfit and roared along on a motorcycle with a band of

Hell's Angel's-type characters. She was the most flamboyant, gorgeous, feisty pig in the world. And so when she was upstaged, it was a particularly hilarious event. Once, for example, while she was singing, another pig leaned backward over a balcony and played a trumpet solo, stealing the spotlight away from Miss Piggy. Jim Henson reportedly hadn't expected that to happen, and he loved it. He constantly encouraged staffers to be creative.

Dave Goelz, one of the people who worked with Jim closely, would one day reminisce: "There are many images of Jim that linger, but one of the strongest is of him standing in front of a big studio monitor with his arms folded in front of him and one hand on his chin, laughing out loud at a playback of another puppeteer's work. Jim Henson was an incredibly generous performer who was able to complement his comrades so that everyone could shine. He always gave due credit."

Kermit once confronted Miss Piggy with a

burning question: Had she placed an item in a gossip column about them being married? She didn't deny it. But she said it was just a little item. Kermit was enraged. The item had, in fact, been featured in a very big way, he said. Then he did a very un-Kermit like thing: He yelled and yelled and fired Miss Piggy. "You're fired! You're fired! You're fired!" She never resolved her conflict between her overwhelming ambition for a career and her desire for a happy love life with Kermit. She constantly pursued him, and she never won him over. His rejection of her gave both of them greater dimension.

The fame of the Muppets continued to grow. By 1977, as *The Muppet Show* backed by Sir Lew Grade went into its second season, Macy's sponsored its first Kermit the Frog balloon. And Jim went on to other projects—movies that he wanted to make. Sir Lew Grade backed him for those, too. Jim and his daughter Cheryl wrote the story for the movie *The Dark Crystal* by 1978. A little later would come *Labyrinth*.

The Muppet Show began its third season in 1978, and *The Muppet Movie*—Jim's first with the Muppets—went into production in Los Angeles. Jim bought a building for his London headquarters the next year, and there he developed *The Dark Crystal* and found a home for his Creature Shop—an outgrowth of his conception for his Muppets. The Creature Shop produced whimsical creatures decidedly more fantastic and weirder to look at than the fuzzy, furry, and feathery Muppets beloved by the children who were fans of *Sesame Street*.

In 1979, Kermit the Frog actually played the host of *The Tonight Show*. That was the stronghold of Johnny Carson, who had become king of the late-night television talk shows. A famed CBS journalism show, *60 Minutes,* did a special report on the Muppets. The first Muppet movie opened in the United States that year. By 1980, the Muppets were appearing everyplace—at the Kennedy Center for the Performing Arts in Washington, D.C.; in a park near Philadelphia;

in a touring show; and in retail stores selling Muppet paraphernalia. A new Muppet movie went into production.

It would be called *The Great Muppet Caper*, starring Miss Piggy as an aspiring fashion model. By 1981, Miss Piggy began to be touted as an author, and her books on such topics as *Miss Piggy's Guide to Life* were published. Then came *The Muppets Take Manhattan*, another movie, with classic production numbers and a real flavor of Manhattan. NASA, the United States space agency, included a tape of the Muppets in a space shuttle mission.

In 1982, Jim Henson established the Henson Foundation to promote public support for the art of puppetry. The Kermitage Collection came into existence; the name "Kermitage" was a play on words: There's a famous Russian art museum in Saint Petersburg called The Hermitage.

And yet another Jim Henson show with a variety of abstract creatures, called *Fraggle Rock*, began its first season of taping in Toronto. Miss

Piggy had her own television special on ABC. And *The Dark Crystal* movie had its premiere.

Each year more Muppet enterprises, shows, and movies went into development and came to fruition. By 1986, yet another new show, *The Storyteller,* based on folktales Jim's daughter Lisa had written in college, started to develop in London. Jim worked tirelessly, always away from home. His son Brian would later say that Jim Henson had many worlds in his head. Because Jim had so little time to spend at home with his family, he took the children with him to his workplaces whenever he could. School vacations gave the Hensons many opportunities to be together. The children, who were growing up, could take jet planes with Jim around the world.

In 1986, too, he and Jane separated legally. The more famous and involved he became in his work, the less time he had for his life with Jane. For him, home was where the project was. Not only did he have several homes in London and the United States, but he had bought a beautiful, historic townhouse with a sweeping central staircase on Manhattan's Upper East Side—117 East 69th Street—to house the New York headquarters of the Henson Company in 1978. Jane continued living in the suburbs. She and Jim remained friends. They never divorced. Friends knew they still had deep feelings for each other. But the demands of Jim's career and the love and time he lavished on all his projects left no space for a conventional marriage.

In a documentary to be made some years later, *The World of Jim Henson,* colleagues would say about him how much he inspired them and how much he pushed them to work harder—and harder. He knew all about struggle. But he was an optimist, and he always said, "It will be okay." His head was always full of plans combining dreams and practicalities. And he had a genius for making the dreams become practical.

One day, at a meeting in London, Jim said to the people working for him, "Let's do a children's show that brings peace to the world."

They thought that was typical of Jim Henson.

In 1987, he was elected to the Television Academy Hall of Fame. By 1989, The Walt Disney Company and Henson Associates, Inc., announced a merger agreement. One of Henson's shows, *Muppet Babies,* began its sixth season on CBS. The Teenage Mutant Ninja Turles were built in London by Jim Henson's Creature Shop. Many of Jim's projects went on full steam ahead at the same time. Some of the Henson children became active participants as puppeteers and writers in his projects. Brian became an experienced puppeteer-performer in his teens.

And *Sesame Street* went into its twentieth year in 1989.

An Unforeseen Disaster

In one *Sesame Street* episode, a famous guest talked to Kermit, asking him how things were going. Kermit answered that life was going along rather smoothly. There had been "no unforeseen disasters," he said. Suddenly a horde of Muppet characters ran across the set and knocked Kermit down several times. The guest mentioned the mess. Kermit, famous for his patience, calmness, and philosophical outlook, downplayed the problem. Everyone thought Kermit's calm, positive

outlook on life mirrored Jim Henson's own attitude exactly. Kermit said softly, "That's a disaster
we knew about all along."

And then an unforeseen disaster happened to
Jim Henson. Friends said that he had been
thinking about his mortality—the certainty of
his dying one day—ever since he turned age
fifty. He had not thought about it much before
then, as far as anyone knew. Actually, fifty is not
an old age. But something about it troubled Jim.
He was taking a vacation on the Côte d'Azur in
France that year when he decided to write a let-
ter to his children. But he didn't want it opened
until he died.

"I'm not at all afraid of the thought of death
and look forward to it," he wrote. "I suggest you
first have a friendly little service of some kind. It
would be lovely if there was a song or two . . .
and someone said some nice, happy words
about me . . . This all may sound silly to you
guys, but what the hell, I'm gone . . . and who
can argue with me?"

By 1990, when he was fifty-three years old, he was still driving himself relentlessly. He was toiling with a project called *Jim Henson's Muppet*Vision 3D* for the Disney-MGM Studios Theme Park at Walt Disney World. He was always flying between New York City, Los Angeles, and Orlando, Florida, at that time. As his agent, Bernie Brillstein, would soon say to reporters, "He belonged to the world."

Then *The Muppets at Disney World* was taped. But the pace was catching up with him. In 1990, Jim Henson, a multimillionaire with houses in London, Malibu, Connecticut, and Orlando, and luxurious, expensive European cars, became very tired. Not only did he work hard, he also enjoyed energy-consuming, leisure-time activities. He went camel riding in Egypt, and hot-air ballooning in France. He also liked simple bike riding. He tried to keep in shape with a rowing machine. He seemed to be bristling with energy. But he looked his age—and more. He had many little lines etched into his kindly face.

On May 4, 1990, he had a sore throat. That day he was a guest on the late-night talk show hosted by Arsenio Hall. A week later, on Saturday, Jim took his daughter Cheryl with him to visit his father and stepmother, Barbara, who was called Bobby, in Ahoskie, North Carolina. Jim's mother, Betty, had died many years earlier. The house, which had a screened-in porch, afforded a quiet place for people to sit down and relax. Jim loved it there, his stepmother later reminsced. The family played croquet that afternoon. Then Cheryl and Jim stayed overnight at a nearby motel. On Sunday morning, he didn't feel like getting out of bed.

He didn't feel like eating lunch, either. In the airport on his way back to New York, he sat down on the side of a radiator. Cheryl became worried and asked him if he was okay.

He said, "I'm just tired." She didn't think that was strange, because he had been working nonstop.

But then he said, "Hi-ho, Kermit the Frog

here." Cheryl thought that was a very unusual remark for him to make. Though many people believed that Kermit the Frog was nearly a carbon copy of Jim's personality, Jim himself said that wasn't true. When he set that Muppet down, it became a lifeless piece of green cloth. And Jim went on to other matters.

Cheryl said, "What, Daddy?"

He returned to his three-bedroom apartment at the fashionable Sherry Netherland Hotel in midtown Manhattan, where he had a beautiful view of Central Park from 59th Street. He was supposed to go to a Muppets recording session, but he canceled the date. That's when Cheryl knew he was really sick. By the next day, she, along with his son John and one of his assistants, visited Jim and tried to get him to eat chicken soup. Someone—perhaps Jim himself—called his wife, Jane. The couple had been separated for years, by then. She arrived at 7 P.M. He asked her to stay overnight. That was unusual. Brian was in London on business.

"We just talked," Jane Henson would later tell a writer for *People* magazine in an article published on June 18, 1990. "There was no division of broken marriage or anything like that. We were just there together."

By the wee hours of the morning, Jim's breathing problems had become so severe that Jane wanted to take him to a hospital. But he didn't want to go. Jane knew that his Christian Science upbringing probably affected his decision. Furthermore, he always liked to see things through for himself. She called him a free spirit. And he wasn't easily alarmed.

But at 4 A.M., Jim Henson changed his mind and let a driver take him to New York Hospital. Doctors discovered he had a rare type of streptococcus pneumonia. They might have been able to cure him with antibiotics if he had gone to the hospital sooner. But it was too late.

He died at age fifty-three on May 16, 1990. His death shocked people and made headlines around the world. The "friendly little service" he had asked his family to provide for him turned out to be a gigantic gathering of five thousand people at the Cathedral of St. John the Divine, an Episcopal church in Morningside Heights, near Columbia University. Many people who had never even met him went to the service.

His children would look back on those days right after his death as a terrible time. They wanted to mourn for their father, and yet they had to take care of the demands of the virtual empire he had left to them and the rest of the world. The children had a hard time at first taking control of the company and steering it well. The merger Jim Henson had made with Disney ended. But Brian was named head of his father's company, and he and his siblings managed to carry on very well. Cheryl was particularly active.

As a child, Jim Henson knew he had wanted to make a difference. He had told that to Jane, she said. He wanted to leave the world a little better place than it was when he got here, she knew and told reporters.

It would turn out that he had written his own best eulogy. In 1986, he had written some notes that were supposed to be included in a book. It was supposed to be called *Courage of Conviction*. But it was never published. However, an excerpt from his notes was published. It said:

Over the years, I've evolved my own set of beliefs and attitudes—as we all have—that I feel works for me.

I believe that life is basically a process of growth—that we go through many lives, choosing those situations and problems that we will learn through. I believe that we form our own lives, that we create our own reality, and that everything works out for the best. I know I drive some people crazy with what seems to be ridiculous optimism, but it has always worked out for me.

I believe in taking a positive attitude toward the world, toward people, and toward my work. I think I'm here for a purpose. I think it's likely that we all are, but I'm only sure about myself. I try to tune myself in to whatever it is that I'm supposed to be, and I try to think of myself as a part of all of us—all mankind and all life. I find it's not easy to keep these lofty thoughts in mind as the day goes by, but it certainly helps me a great deal to start out this way.

I love my work, and because I enjoy it, it doesn't really feel like work. Thus I spend most of my time working. I like working collaboratively with people. At its best, the film and television world functions creatively this way. I have a terrific group of people who work with me, and I think of the work that we do as "our" work. . . .

I find that it's very important for me to stop every now and then and get recharged and reinspired. The beauty of nature has been one of the great inspirations in my life. Growing up as an artist, I've always been in awe of the incredible beauty of every last bit of design in nature. The wonderful color schemes of nature, which always work harmoniously, are particularly dazzling to me. I love to lie in an open field looking up at the sky. One of my happiest moments of inspiration came to me many years ago as I lay on the grass, looking up into the leaves and branches of a big old tree in California. I remember feeling very much a part of everything and everyone.

Working as I do with the movement of puppet creatures, I'm always struck by the feebleness of our efforts to achieve naturalistic movement. Just looking at the incredible movement of a lizard or a bird, or even the smallest insect, can be a very humbling experience. . . .

When I was young, my ambition was to be one of the people who made a difference in this world. My hope still is to leave the world a little bit better for my having been here.

It's a wonderful life and I love it.

Jim was honored repeatedly throughout the following years. He had his star added to the Hollywood Walk of Fame in 1991.

In 1992, the Joseph Papp's Public Theater in New York City presented the First New York International Festival of Puppet Theater, a production of the Jim Henson Foundation.

In 1993, Kermit the Frog appeared at President Bill Clinton's inaugural festivities.

And the momentum of the Muppets kept going unabated with Jim Henson's children at the helm, carrying on the powerful legacy. In the family business headquarters in Manhattan, there's even a Kermit the Frog telephone in the lobby, and many awards in a glass case to show off the prestige that the fellow from the little Mississippi Delta town achieved. There's also a

Muppets museum in Leland, Mississippi, where Kermit the Frog has his roots.

Lisa, Heather, and John Henson are members of the board of the family company. Cheryl Henson, a vice president of Jim Henson Productions, works with *Sesame Street* and runs the Jim Henson Foundation. Brian Henson is president of Jim Henson Productions and head of the family company.

Sesame Street was thirty years old as it headed for the year 2000. Muppets were still making commercials and movies. Muppets were everywhere, and they kept bringing joy to the world. Jim Henson had left the world a better place.

For Further Reading

Among several books for children about Jim Henson are:

1. *The Art of the Muppets.* New York: A Muppet Press/Bantam Book, 1980. This is a retrospective of twenty-five years of the Muppets prepared by the staff of Henson Associates.

2. *Meet Jim Henson,* by Susan Canizares and Samantha Berger. New York: Scholastic, Inc., 1999. This simple, illustrated booklet for young readers was prepared with the cooperation of the Henson Company.

For adults, an excellent book is:

Jim Henson: The Works, by Christopher Finch. New York: Random House, 1993. This illustrated, detailed book covers Jim Henson's entire career.

These books contain very little information about his childhood before he moved to Hyattsville, Maryland. Almost all that information comes from the author's interviews with people who grew up, or knew Jim Henson, in Stoneville and Leland, Mississippi.